PEOPLE OF DARKNESS

➤Books by TONY HILLERMAN

Fiction

A Thief of Time
Skinwalkers
The Ghostway
The Dark Wind
People of Darkness
Listening Woman
Dance Hall of the Dead
The Fly on the Wall
The Blessing Way
The Boy Who Made
    Dragonfly *(for children)*

Nonfiction

The Great Taos Bank Robbery
Rio Grande
New Mexico
The Spell of New Mexico

Tony Hillerman

PEOPLE OF DARKNESS

PERENNIAL LIBRARY

Harper & Row, Publishers, New York
Cambridge, Philadelphia, San Francisco, London
Mexico City, São Paulo, Singapore, Sydney

A hardcover edition of this book was originally published in 1980 by Harper & Row, Publishers.

PEOPLE OF DARKNESS. Copyright © 1980 by Tony Hillerman. All rights reserved. Printed in the United States of America. No part of this book may be used or reproduced in any manner whatsoever without written permission except in the case of brief quotations embodied in critical articles and reviews. For information address Harper & Row, Publishers, Inc., 10 East 53rd Street, New York, N.Y. 10022. Published simultaneously in Canada by Fitzhenry & Whiteside Limited, Toronto.

First PERENNIAL LIBRARY edition published 1988.

Library of Congress Cataloging-in-Publication Data

Hillerman, Tony.
  People of darkness / Tony Hillerman.—1st Perennial
  Library ed.

     p. cm.
  ISBN 0-06-080950-7
  1. Navaho Indians—Fiction.   I. Title.
PS3558.I45P4   1988
813'.54—dc19
                                                    88-21189
                                                    CIP

    89 90 91 92 OPM 10 9 8 7 6 5 4 3

PEOPLE OF
DARKNESS

1

IT WAS A JOB which required waiting for cultures to grow, for toxins to develop, for antibodies to form, for reagents to react. And while she waited, the bacteriologist would roll her wheelchair to the windows and look down upon the world. The world below was the parking lot of the Cancer Research and Treatment Center, the neighbor of the bacteriologist's Communicable Disease Laboratory on the University of New Mexico North Campus. It was a crowded lot, and a competitive one, and somewhere in the second year of watching it, the bacteriologist found herself familiar with its patterns. She knew when the meter maids made their rounds, and how long it usually took the tow truck to arrive, and what sort of violation provoked this ultimate punishment, and which vehicles tended to park illegally. She even knew of a romance which seemed to have flared between the female owner of a Datsun and the male owner of the blue Mercedes convertible that parked in the space reserved for one of the lofty administrators. Somewhere in that same second year she had started bringing her binoculars to the lab. She had finally left them there. They were in her hands now—focused upon a dirty green pickup truck which was nosing its way hesitatingly into a space guarded by a sign that read:

RESERVED FOR ASSOCIATE DIRECTOR
VIOLATORS WILL BE TOWED AT OWNERS EXPENSE

The bacteriologist had learned long ago that cancer patients tended to be scofflaws. They were dying and they knew it. In the face of that, other considerations became less important. But habits of civilized behavior still generally prevailed. It was rare to see such open defiance as the pickup was now demonstrating.

The defiant one was male, an Indian. Through the binoculars he didn't look defiant. He looked stolid and sick. He climbed laboriously from the cab. The bacteriologist noticed a suitcase on the passenger's seat and felt a sudden mild thrill of admiration. He was checking himself in, abandoning his truck forever to the mercies of the law. The nose thumbed at fate. But the Indian left the suitcase behind.

He was a large man, with the heavy torso and slender hips the bacteriologist had learned to identify with Navajos. He wore jeans and—despite the August heat—a denim jacket. He walked slowly toward the patients' entrance—a sick man's walk. He'll check himself in, the bacteriologist thought, and then he'll come back and get the suitcase, and move the truck.

Now there was another vehicle showing equally blatant illegality. It was a Chevrolet, silver-gray and new, which rolled past the green pickup and came to rest in the space reserved for the CRTC director. The driver's door opened and a slender man emerged, dressed in white, a straw hat pushed back on his head. The man stood for a moment, apparently looking at the pickup truck. Then he walked around his car and opened the door on the passenger's side. He leaned in, apparently working on something on the front seat. Finally he lifted out a grocery sack with its top folded down. He placed it on the bed of the pickup, among the boards and boxes against the cab. That done, he looked around him, studying the parking lot, the sidewalks, staring finally directly toward the bacteriologist. He was very blond, she saw. Almost an albino. Within a minute he was back in the gray Chevy, driving slowly away.

It was almost noon when the bacteriologist determined that the life form that had reproduced itself in her petri dish was not a food-poisoning salmonella but harmless nonpathogenic *Escherichia coli.* She made the required notes, completed the report, and pushed her chair back to the window. A tow truck had arrived. The bacteriologist focused her binoculars. The driver's helper was completing the attachment of the towing bar to the rear of the green pickup. He waved his left hand and squatted beside the pickup wheel, watching something. The sound of the tow truck winch was lost to distance and insulated glass. But the bacteriologist could see the rear of the pickup begin to rise.

Abruptly, all vision was lost in a dazzle of light. The sound came a second later—a cannon-shot boom. The glass on the bacteriologist's window was pressed inward to its tolerance and just beyond; it cracked, then flexed violently outward, where its shards joined those of a hundred other windows raining down on the empty sidewalks below.

2

THE RAIN CONVERTED ITSELF abruptly into a flurry of popcorn snow. It rattled off Jim Chee's uniform hat, bounced down the collar of his uniform jacket, and made him shiver. It was the third day of November by the First National Bank of Grants calendar back on Chee's desk, and the very beginning of the Season When the Thunder Sleeps by the less rigid traditional calendar of the Dinee. By either calendar it was too early for this sort of weather—even at this mile-and-a-half altitude on the slope of Mount Taylor. Howard Morgan had predicted possible snow flurries on his Channel 7 weathercast, but Chee hadn't believed it. He'd left his winter coat back at the police station.

He glanced at his vehicle—a white Chevrolet with the seal of the Navajo Nation and the legend NAVAJO TRIBAL POLICE blazoned on its door. He could retire to the car and turn on the heater. He could seek shelter at the entryway of the residence of Benjamin J. Vines, and perhaps ring the bell a few more times in the hope of attracting someone. The bell made an odd singing sound which he could hear echoing pleasantly through the heavy door. While it had attracted no response at all, Chee was tempted to ring it again just to hear it. The third alternative was to turn up the collar of his jacket to ward off the sleet and continue satisfying his curiosity about this house. It had been designed, so he'd heard, by Frank Lloyd Wright, and was reputed to be the most expensive home in New Mexico. Chee's curiosity about it, as about all things in the white man's world, was intense. It was all the more intense at the moment because he might very soon enter that strange world. By December 10, less than five weeks away, he had to decide whether he would accept an appointment to the FBI, and a place in the world of singing doorbells.

He pulled his jacket collar around his neck, and folded down his hat brim, and continued his inspection. Chee was standing beside a semidetached triple garage. Like the house itself, it was built of native granite, linked to the structure by a low, curving wall of the same material. Just behind the wall, in a grassy plot no more than fifteen feet long, two small markers of black marble held Chee's attention. Gravestones. He leaned over the wall. The name chiseled into the one just to the right of where Chee stood was DILLON CHARLEY. Under it, the legend read:

He Didn't Remember When He Was Born
Died December 11, 1953
A Good Indian

Chee grinned. Was the sardonic double meaning intended? Was Vines, or whoever had ordered this legend carved, familiar with General Sheridan's dictum that the only good Indian was a dead Indian? The stone to Chee's left read:

MRS. BENJAMIN J. VINES (ALICE)
Born April 13, 1909
Died June 4, 1949
A Faithful Woman

Faithful to B. J. Vines? It seemed an odd thing to put on a tombstone, but then everything about the white man's burial customs seemed odd to Chee. The Navajos lacked this sentimentality about corpses. Death robbed the body of its value. Even its identity was lost with the departing *chindi*. What the ghost left behind was something to be disposed of with a minimum risk of contamination to the living. The names of the dead were left unspoken, certainly not carved in stone.

Chee glanced again at the Charley tombstone. The name tugged at memory. There were no Charleys in Chee's clan—the Slow Talking Dinee—and none among the other clans that occupied the Rough Rock country of his family. But here on the east margin of the reservation—among the Salt Dinee, and the Many Goats Dinee, and the Mud Clan, and the Standing Rock Clan—the name seemed fairly common. And somebody named Charley had done something recently which he should be able to remember.

"Does it seem an unusual place for a graveyard?"

The voice came from behind him. A woman, perhaps in her mid fifties, with a thin, handsome, unsmiling face. She was wearing a coat of some expensive fur over jeans. A navy knit cap covered her ears. "It's one of B.J.'s little eccentricities, burying people by the garage. Are you Sergeant Chee?"

"Jim Chee," Chee said. The woman was looking at him, frowning critically, making no offer to shake his hand.

"You're younger than I expected," she said. "They told me you were an authority on your religion. Could that be right?"

"I'm learning to be a *yataalii*," Chee said. He used the Navajo word because no English word really expressed it. The anthropologists called them shamans, and most people around the reservation called them singers, or medicine men, and none of these expressions really fit the role he would play for his people if he ever finished learning to play it. "Are you Mrs. Vines?" he asked.

"Of course," the woman said. "Rosemary Vines." She glanced at the tombstone. "The second Mrs. Vines. But let's get out of this sleet."

The house had puzzled Chee. Its front wall was a sweeping, virtually windowless curve, suggesting a natural formation of stone. But inside the massive entry doors and through the entry foyer the puzzle solved itself. The front was actually the back. The ceiling rose in a soaring curve toward a great wall of glass. Beyond the wall, the mountain slope fell away. Now the view was obscured by clouds and gusts of sleet, but on the usual day Chee knew the glass over-looked immense space—across the Laguna and Acoma Indian reservations to the south and east, southward across the forty-mile sea of cooled lava called the malpais toward the Zuni Mountains, and eastward across the Cañoncito Reservation to the great blue hump of the Sandia Mountains behind Albuquerque. The room was almost as spectacular as the view. A fireplace dominated the native-stone in-terior wall to Chee's left, with the pelt of a polar bear on the carpet by the hearth. On the wall to his right, a hundred glassy eyes stared from trophy heads. Chee stared back: water buffalo, impala, wildebeest, ibex, oryx, elk, mule deer, and a dozen species he couldn't name.

"It takes some getting used to," Mrs. Vines said. "But at least he keeps all the fierce-looking ones in his trophy room. These are the ones that couldn't bite back."

"I had heard he was a famous hunter," Chee said. "Didn't he win the Weatherby Trophy?"

"Twice," Rosemary Vines said. "In 1962 and 1971. Those were bad years for anything with fang, fur, or feathers." She draped the mink over the back of a sofa. Under it she wore a man's plaid shirt. She was a trim woman, one who took care of her body. But there was a tension about her. It showed in her face, in the way she held herself, in the taut muscles along her narrow jaw. Her hands twisted together at her belt line.

"I'll have a drink," Mrs. Vines said. "Join me?"

"No, thank you," Chee said.

"Coffee?"

"If it's no trouble."

Mrs. Vines spoke into the grillwork beside the fireplace. "Maria." The grille buzzed in response.

"Bring a Scotch and some coffee."

She turned back to Chee. "You're an experienced investigator. That's right, isn't it?" she asked. "And you're stationed at Crownpoint and you know everything about the Navajo religion."

"I was transferred to Crownpoint this year," Chee said, "and I know something about the customs of my people." This was not the time to tell this arrogant white woman that the Navajos had no religion in the white man's meaning of the term (in fact, had no word in their language for religion). First he would find out what she wanted with him.

"Sit down," Rosemary Vines said. She gestured toward a huge blue sofa and seated herself in a chair of stainless-steel tubing and polished leather.

"Do you also understand witchcraft?" She perched at the edge of the chair, smiling, tense, her hands twisting now in her lap. "That business about Navajo Wolves, or skinwalkers, or whatever you call them. Do you know all about that?"

"Something," Chee said.

"I'll want to hire you, then," Rosemary Vines said. "You have some accrued annual leave coming. . . ." An elderly woman—a Pueblo Indian, but Chee wasn't sure which Pueblo—came in with a tray. Mrs. Vines took her glass—from its color, more Scotch than water—and Chee accepted his coffee. The Indian woman examined him from the corner of her eye with shy curiosity. "You have thirty days' leave time," Mrs. Vines continued. "That should be more than enough."

For what? Chee thought. But he didn't say it. His mother had taught him one learns through the ear and not the tongue.

"We had a burglary here," Mrs. Vines said. "Someone broke in, they got into B.J.'s quarters and stole a box of his keepsakes. I want to hire you to get it back. B.J.'s at a hospital in Houston. I want it back before he gets home. I'll pay you five hundred dollars now and twenty-five hundred dollars when you return the box. If you don't get it back, you don't get the twenty-five hundred dollars. That's fair enough."

"You can have the sheriff do it for you for free," Chee said. "What does the sheriff say about it?"

"Gordo Sena," Mrs. Vines said. "B.J. has no use for Sena. Nor do I. B.J. wouldn't want him involved in any way. Besides, what good would it do? They'd send out some ignorant deputy. He'd ask a lot of questions and look around and then he'd go away and that would be the end of it." She sipped Scotch. "There's absolutely nothing for the police to go on."

"I'm police," Chee said.

"It will be simple enough for you," Mrs. Vines said. "The People of Darkness stole the box. You find them and get it back."

Chee felt swallowed by the sofa, engulfed in velvety royal-blue comfort. He considered what Mrs. Vines had said, seeking some sense in it. Her eyes were studying him. One of her hands held the glass. The ice moved in the trembling liquid. The other hand fidgeted on the denim of her jean leg. Sleet rattled and scratched at the plate-glass window. Beyond the glass, night was coming.

"The People of Darkness," Chee said.

"Yes," said Rosemary Vines. "It must have been them. Did I tell you nothing was taken except the box? Look around you." She gestured at the room. "They didn't take the silver, or the paintings, or anything else. Just the box. They came to get it. And they took it."

The silver service was on the sideboard—a great urn and a dozen goblets on a massive tray. Worth a lot, Chee thought. And behind it, on the wall, a perfect little Navajo *yei* rug which on the reservation would bring two thousand dollars from the greediest of traders.

Chee resisted an impulse to ask Mrs. Vines what she meant by "People of Darkness." He'd never heard of them. But it would be smarter to simply let her talk.

She talked, perched on the edge of the chair, sipping occasionally. She said that when she had come to this place—the house then still under construction—the foreman of the B. J. Vines ranch had been a Navajo named Dillon Charley—the man now buried next to Vines' first wife by the garage. Vines and Charley had been friends, Rosemary Vines said. "The old man had organized himself some sort of church," Mrs. Vines said. "B.J. was interested in it. Or seemed to be. He claimed he wasn't; said he was just humoring the old man. But he was interested. I'd hear the two of them talking about it. And I know B.J. contributed money. And when you Navajo Police were arresting them, B.J. helped get them out of jail."

"Arresting them?" Chee asked. Understanding dawned. "Was it for using peyote?" If it was, Dillon Charley's cult was part of the Native American Church. It had flourished on the Checkerboard Reservation after World War II, and had been outlawed by the Tribal Council because of its use of the psychedelic drug in its ritual; but the federal court had thrown the tribal law out on grounds that it violated freedom of religion.

"Peyote. Yes. That was it," Rosemary Vines said. "Drug abuse." Her voice was scornful. "B.J. is never discriminating in his interests. Anyway, B.J. gave them some sort of thing out of that precious box of his. He and Dillon Charley had the box out several times. And whatever it was seemed to be very important to their religion. And now they've stolen it."

"What was in the box?" Chee asked.

Mrs. Vines took a drink. "Just keepsakes," she said.

"Like what?" Chee asked. "Anything valuable? What was it these people wanted?"

"I've never seen the inside of that goddamned box," Rosemary Vines said. She laughed. "B.J. has his little secrets. He has his private side, just as I have." Her tone said this was a source of an old resentment. "B.J. called it his keepsake box, and he said nothing in it was worth anything to anyone but him." She laughed again. "Obviously wrong about that."

"Do you have any idea what he gave Dillon Charley out of the box? Any idea at all?"

She looked over the glass at him, her expression wry. "Would moles make any sense?"

Now Chee laughed. This conversation, more and more, reminded him of his very favorite tale from the white culture: *Alice in Wonderland.*

No," he said. "Moles wouldn't make any sense to me."

"What's your word for moles?"

"Dine'etse-tle," Chee said. He pronounced the series of gutturals.

She nodded. "That's what Dillon Charley called it," she said. "I asked him what B.J. had given him and that's what he said. We had a Navajo maid then—that was back when Navajos would work for B.J.—and I asked her what the word meant, and she said 'moles.' "

"That's right," Chee said. Technically, when broken into its parts, it meant more than that. *"Dinee"* was the word for "people." The expression literally meant "people of darkness."

"Why do you call Dillon Charley's church the 'People of Darkness'?" he asked her.

"That's what B.J. called them. Or something like that. It's been so many years, it's hard to remember."

But you do remember, Chee thought. He said, "There's another possible motive for taking that box. This is a legendary place." He motioned around the room. "B. J. Vines is a legendary person. So maybe there's a legend about his keepsake box. Maybe there's a rumor that he keeps it full of gold, or diamonds, or thousand-dollar bills. So somebody who came to take it wouldn't be interested in paintings, or silver, or Navajo rugs. Was it locked? Would they have to carry it out and break it open before they could find out what was in it?"

"It was always locked," Rosemary Vines said. "You'd have thought B.J. kept the crown jewels in it. But B.J. said it was just mementos, odds and ends to remember. I don't think he was lying." She smiled her taut, humorless smile. "B.J. is very big about saving keepsakes. He saves everything. If he can't frame it, he stuffs it." The humorless smile became a humorless chuckle. "You'd think he was afraid of losing his memory."

"But an outsider . . ."

"An outsider wouldn't have known where B.J. kept it," Mrs. Vines said. Her voice was impatient. "Dillon Charley knew. I can only presume that Dillon told his son." She rose, a graceful motion. "Come along and I'll show you."

Chee followed her. "One more point," he said. "Your husband knows all about this People of Darkness business. Wouldn't he rather go after the box himself?"

"I said he was at a hospital," Mrs. Vines said. "He had a stroke last summer. Away hunting in Alaska. They flew him back. He's partly paralyzed on his left side. They're fitting him with a device in Houston so he can get around better, but I don't want him chasing after burglars."

"No," Chee agreed.

She paused at an open doorway which led off the hall, motioning Chee past her. "He's the kind who would, crutches and all," she said. "He'd try to go after them in an iron lung. That's why I want the box back right away. I want it back when he gets home. I don't want him worrying about it."

The room that Rosemary Vines called "B.J.'s office" was down a carpeted hallway. It was large, with a beamed ceiling, a stone fireplace flanked by windows that looked across the mountain slope, and a great glass-surfaced desk. Three of the walls were covered with the heads of cats, each snarling in terminal rage. Chee's glance took in three lions, two lionesses, four tigers, and a variety of panthers, leopards, pumas, cheetahs, and predator cats which Chee could not identify. In all, forty or fifty, he guessed. The light reflected from hundreds of bared teeth.

"The burglar came through that window beside

the fireplace and he went directly to the place where B.J. kept the box and he took it. He didn't disturb anything else," Rosemary Vines said. "He knew where it was." She looked at Chee. "Would you?"

Chee examined the room. Rosemary Vines had said her husband collected mementos. He did indeed. The room was cluttered with them. The west wall, the only one free of Vines' array of trophy predators, was a gallery of photographs and framed certificates. Vines beside a dead tiger. Vines at the controls of a speedboat. Vines holding a trophy. Vines dwarfed by the wheel of one of those immense ore trucks at the Red Deuce Mine. Vines' broad, gray-bearded face beaming under a pith helmet. His narrower, younger, black-bearded face peering out the cockpit window of a plane. Chee glanced away from the gallery of Vineses. Two glass-fronted cabinets, one crowded with trophies and cups, the other with carved and sculpted items of wood and stone. Shelves, a table, every flat surface carrying its burden of the artifacts of memory. Mrs. Vines was watching him, her face amused. "All those *objets d'art* are his sculpture," she said. She gestured toward the gallery of photographs. "And as you can see, my husband has a problem with his ego."

"Would it have been in the desk?" Chee asked.

"Wrong," Mrs. Vines said. She walked to the fireplace wall and lifted down the head of the smallest tiger. Behind it, a metal panel swung slightly open, one corner bent.

"They knew where to look, and they knew they

had to bring something to pry this door open, and that's exactly what they did," Mrs. Vines said. "Didn't even bother to shut the panel, or hang the head back up."

Chee inspected the panel. It was mounted on heavy hinges and secured with a lock that looked expensive. Whoever had opened it had jammed something like a crowbar between panel and frame and pried until the lock gave. The door was thick and surprisingly heavy on its hinges, but it hadn't been strong enough to withstand the leverage. Chee was mildly surprised. The door looked stronger than it was.

"How big was the box?" Chee asked.

"Just about the size of that empty space," Mrs. Vines said. "B.J. had it made. It had the knob of a combination lock in the front of it. What I want you to do is find those people, and tell them unless they give it back—and everything that was inside of it— I'll make damn sure they go to prison for it." She moved to the doorway and motioned Chee out ahead of her. "You might also tell them B.J. will put a spell on them if he gets home and finds that box gone."

"What?" Chee said.

Mrs. Vines laughed. "The Navajos around here think he's a witch," she said.

"I had the impression that he got along well with the Dinee," Chee said.

"That was a long time ago. Dillon Charley died and that was the end of getting along with Navajos. Within a year or two nearly every one of them who was working here had quit. We haven't had one of your people on the payroll for years. Maria is an Acoma. Most of the hired hands are Lagunas or Acomas."

"What happened?"

"I honestly don't know," Mrs. Vines said. "I'm sure it was something B.J. did, but God knows what. I asked Maria, and she said the Navajos think B.J. is bad luck."

"And you haven't reported this burglary to the sheriff?"

"Gordo Sena would do absolutely nothing for us," Mrs. Vines said. "B.J. got him beaten for reelection once, many years ago, and tried it a couple of times since. Sena's not an honest man, and I don't want him involved with this in any way whatsoever."

"I'm going to have to report it," Chee said. "I have to get along with the sheriff. We're in the same line of work."

"Go ahead," Mrs. Vines said. "If he sends someone out, I'll tell him we're not signing a complaint and not pressing charges and it was all a mistake."

Chee retrieved his hat from the sofa. It was damp.

"The man you want to find is old Dillon Charley's son. He took over the church. His name's Emerson Charley and he lives around Grants somewhere. He used to come around here some after his father died and get into arguments with B.J."

"About what?"

"I think he wanted whatever was in the box," Mrs. Vines said. "I heard him say something about having their luck locked up in it. Something like that. I remember hearing old Dillon saying about the same thing. He was laughing about it, but Emerson wasn't laughing."

Chee revolved his hat on his hands, looking thoughtful.

"Two more questions," he said. "How would Emerson Charley have known about the safe?"

"That's easy," Rosemary Vines said. "Dillon knew about it. Dillon was in here with B.J. a lot. I'm sure Dillon told his boy about it. After all, Emerson was going to keep Dillon's crazy cult going. What's the other question?"

"How did Dillon Charley die?"

"How?" Mrs. Vines looked puzzled. Then she laughed. "Oh," she said. "I see what you're thinking. Nothing mysterious. He died of cancer." She laughed again. "That's the reason for that strange line on the tombstone about him being a good Indian. He'd been sick and he came back from Albuquerque one day and told B.J. that the doctor told him he couldn't be cured. He told B.J. the doctor told him he was going to be a good Indian in a couple of months." Rosemary Vines grimaced. "Laughing at his own death—that's the sort of weird thing that impressed B.J. He put it on the tombstone." She handed him an envelope.

"I'm going to have to talk to my office about this," Chee said. "And give it some thought. I'll let you know in a couple of days. Maybe I'll return this."

"Your superiors will approve," Mrs. Vines said. "I already checked on that."

"I'll call you," Chee said.

The old woman from Acoma opened the front door for Chee and held it against the gusting wind. He nodded to her as he stepped into the darkness.

"Tenga cuidado," the old woman said.

It occurred to Chee as he started the cold engine that she couldn't speak Navajo, and he wouldn't understand her Keresan language, and that it would have been more logical of her to say "Be careful" in English instead of Spanish, which he might not understand. Then it occurred to him that perhaps Mrs. Vines did not speak Spanish, and that the warning might not have anything to do with the weather.

3

BY THE TIME CHEE had made his cautious way down the mountain and into Grants, the storm had moved away to the east. It left behind an air mass which was windless, arid, and twenty degrees below freezing. It also left a half-inch layer of snow as light and dry as feathers. Chee detoured past the Valencia County Office Building on the chance that the tricky road conditions would have the Sheriff's Department working late. The light was on. He pulled into the parking lot.

Except for the east, the clouds were gone now and the night sky, swept clean of dust, was ablaze with starlight. Chee stood for a moment, enjoying it. He hunted out the autumn constellations—the formations that rose from the south as the earth tilted to end summer and begin the Season When the Thunder Sleeps. Chee knew them not by the names the Greeks and Romans had given them, but from his grandfather. Now he picked out the Spider Woman (named Aquarius by the Romans), low on the southern horizon, and the mischievous Blue Flint Boys, whom the Greeks called the Pleiades, just above the blackness of the storm against the northeast sky. Almost directly overhead was Born of Water, the philosophical member of the Hero Twins. Over his right shoulder, surrounded by stars of lesser magnitude, soared the Blue Heron. According to the Origin Myth as told in Chee's clan, it had been the Heron whom First Man had sent back into the flooding underworld to rescue the forgotten witchcraft bundle and thus bring evil into the surface world. Chee felt the cold seeping under his collar and through his pant legs. He hurried into the warmth of the county building.

The third door down the hall bore the legend LAWRENCE SENA, SHERIFF. VALENCIA COUNTY. WALK IN. The capitalized LAW, Chee had heard, represented Sena's effort to replace "Gordo" with a less insulting nickname. It hadn't worked. Chee turned the doorknob, hoping that Sena had left a deputy handling the overtime. He had met the sheriff only once, making a courtesy call after his transfer to Crownpoint. Sena had impressed him as being hard, smart, and abrasive—like Mrs. Vines, moved beyond the need for tact by access to power. Perhaps it was the product of having too much money, Chee thought. Uranium. Vines had found it, and had sold his leases for a fortune and an interest in the huge open pit mine called the Red Deuce. The Sena family's fortune was the accident of scratching a living on a worn-out ranch which happened to have radioactive ore twenty feet below the cactus roots. Ah, well, Chee thought, such a rich man would be at home on a night like this.

Sheriff Sena was standing in a glassed-in cubicle which insulated the department's radio operator from the world. He was listening while a middle-aged woman wearing headphones argued with someone about dispatching a wrecker somewhere. A long moment passed before he noticed Chee.

"Yeah," he said. "What can I do for you, Sergeant?"

"I want to report a burglary," Chee said.

Sheriff Sena registered the mildest form of surprise by lifting his heavy black eyebrows a fraction of a millimeter. His black eyes rested on Chee's face, bland and neutral, waiting for an explanation.

"Somebody got into B.J. Vines' house and stole his lockbox," Chee said. "Nothing very valuable. Just keepsakes."

Sena's eyes were watchful. "Well," he said finally. "That's interesting." He moved past Chee out of the cubicle. "Come on in to my desk and I'll get my pencil."

The sheriff's office was a room even smaller than the radio cubicle—barely large enough for a desk with a swivel chair on one side of it and a wooden kitchen chair on the other.

Sena eased his bulk into the swivel and looked up at Chee. "I guess Vines broke his telephone," Sena said. "Is that why he didn't report it himself?"

"Vines is away," Chee said. "His wife told me she

didn't report it because she didn't see how the police could solve it."

Sena pulled open the top desk drawer and extracted a pencil and a pad. "Couldn't solve it," he said. "She say why?"

"Nothing to go on," Chee said.

"Have a seat," Sena said, indicating the chair. The years and the weather had engraved Sena's round face with a thousand expressive lines. They expressed skepticism.

"She didn't say anything about old B.J. not having any use for me?"

Chee smiled. "I think she mentioned something about you two not being friendly. I don't remember exactly how she put it."

"How come she told you about the burglary? You a friend of the Vineses?"

"She wants to hire me to get the box back," Chee said.

"Oh," Sena said. The eyebrows rose again, asking why.

"She thinks an Indian did it. A Navajo. That it's got something to do with religion, or witchcraft. Something like that."

Sena thought about it. "Just the lockbox, that right? Nothing else missing?"

"That's what she told me."

"Most likely somebody figured he kept his money in it," Sena said.

"Probably," Chee said.

"But she don't think it's that simple," Sena said.

It was a statement, not a question, and Chee didn't answer it.

He was looking at a framed photograph on the wall behind the sheriff. It seemed to be a disaster scene, twisted steel wreckage in the foreground, a burned-out truck on its side, two men in khaki uniforms looking at something outside the frame, a police car and an ambulance of 1950 vintage. The scene of an explosion, apparently. A small white card stuck in the corner of the frame bore six typed names—all apparently Navajo. Victims, perhaps. The picture was grainy black-and-white, and glass and card were dusty. Sena inserted the pencil eraser between his teeth, leaned back in the swivel chair, and stared at Chee. The sheriff moved his jaw and the pencil waved slowly up and down, an antenna seeking logic. Sena removed it. "What else did she say?"

Chee described the hiding place for the box and how it had been pried open. "Nothing else was missing," he said. "Lots of valuable stuff in the house—right in plain view. Silver. Rugs. Paintings. Worth a lot of money."

"I imagine so," Sena said. "Vines has got more money than Saudi Arabia. What'd she say about religion?"

Chee told him, outlining briefly Mrs. Vines' account of her husband's interest in the church of Dillon Charley, her speculation that something in the box was important to the cult, and that only Charley had known where the box was kept.

"Dillon Charley's a long time dead," Sena said.

"Mrs. Vines said he had a son. She figured he'd told his son about it years ago, and the son decided to come and get it."

Sena sat immobile, studying Chee. "That what she figured?"

"That's what she told me."

"The son's name is Emerson Charley," Sena said. "That ring a bell?"

"Faintly," Chee said. "But I can't place him."

"Remember that killing they had in Albuquerque in August? Somebody put a bomb in a pickup and it killed a couple of fellows in a tow truck trying to haul the pickup away. That was Emerson Charley's pickup."

Chee recalled having read about it. It was a puzzling case. "I remember it," Chee said. "Understand they think the bomb was intended for one of the big shots at the hospital. Divorce settlement or argument or something, from what I heard."

"That's what the Albuquerque police seem to think," Sena said. His tone was skeptical.

"Anyway, Mrs. Vines figures Emerson got the box. She wants me to get it back from him."

"Emerson didn't get the box," Sena said. He reinserted the pencil and chewed on it. His eyes were on Chee, but his attention was far away. He sighed, shook his head, scratched his left sideburn with a thick forefinger. "Emerson's in the hospital," Sena said. "BCMC in Albuquerque. If he's not dead, that is. Last I heard, he was in bad shape."

"I thought he didn't get hurt," Chee said.

"He was already hurt," Sena said. "He'd gone to the hospital to check into that Cancer Research and Treatment Center the university has there. The son of a bitch is dying of cancer." He focused on Chee again, and emitted a snort of ironic laughter. "The APD and the FBI between 'em couldn't figure out why anyone would blow up a Navajo when he's already dying."

"Can you?" Chee asked.

The pencil waved, up and down, up and down. "No," said Sena, "I can't. Not a thing. Did Mrs. Vines say anything to you about some people they used to call the People of Darkness?"

Sena made the question sound casual.

"She mentioned it," Chee said.

"What did she say?" The sheriff's voice, despite his efforts, was tense.

"Not much," Chee said. He repeated what Rosemary Vines had told him about her husband's interest in Dillon Charley's church, about his contributing money, helping members when they were arrested, and giving Charley something "lucky" from the box—perhaps a talisman, Chee guessed. Halfway through it, Sena stifled a yawn. But his eyes weren't sleepy. "Like she said herself, it was all pretty vague," Chee concluded.

Sena yawned again. "Well, I'll send somebody out tomorrow or so and get all the details. No use wasting your time." Sena examined the pencil top. "You weren't figuring on taking that job, were you?"

"Hadn't really decided," Chee said. "Probably not."

"That'd be the best," Sena said. "It was like I was telling you that day you first came in here and introduced yourself—that first week you replaced old Henry Becenti. Like I was telling you then, this jurisdiction business can be a real problem if you ain't careful with it."

"I guess so," Chee said. As far as he could remember, jurisdiction hadn't been discussed during that brief meeting. He was sure it hadn't been.

"I don't know if you ever worked out here on the Checkerboard Reservation before," Sena said. "You're driving along and one minute you're on the Navajo reservation and the next minute you're in Valencia County jurisdiction and usually there's no way in God's world to know the difference. It can be a real problem."

"I bet," Chee said. The Navajo Police lived with jurisdiction problems. Even on the Big Reservation, which sprawled larger than all New England across the borders of New Mexico, Arizona, and Utah, jurisdiction was always a question. The serious felony brought in the FBI. If the suspect was non-Navajo, other questions were raised. Or the crime might lap into the territory of New Mexico State Police, Utah or Arizona Highway Patrol, or involve the Law and Order Division of the Bureau of Indian Affairs. Or even a Hopi constable, or Southern Ute Tribal Police, or an officer of the Jicarilla Apache tribe, or any of a dozen county sheriffs of the three states. But here on the southwestern fringe of the reservation, checkerboarding complicated the problem. In the 1880s, the government deeded every other square mile in a sixty-mile-wide strip to the Atlantic and Pacific Railroad to subsidize extension of its trunk line westward. The A&P had become the Santa Fe generations ago, and the Navajo Nation had gradually bought back part of this looted portion of its Dinetah, its homeland, but in many places this checkerboard pattern of ownership persisted.

"Tell you the truth, Becenti and I had us some trouble when he first took over the Crownpoint station. The Tribal Council had just passed itself a law outlawing peyote, and they were cracking down on the church. You old enough to remember that?"

"I knew about it," Chee said.

"Old Henry got pretty carried away with that," Sena said. "He got so interested in rounding up the peyoteheads that he'd forget where the reservation boundary was and he'd get over into my territory. So I had my boys arrest some of his boys and one thing and another, and finally we got together here and worked out a way so we wouldn't interfere in one another's business." Sena's eyes were intent on Chee's face, making sure he'd understood the lesson.

"I'd think enforcing that peyote ban would have been Lieutenant Becenti's business," Chee said.

"Normally," Sena said, "yes. This time, though, we were looking into another crime and Henry was messing us up." Sena wiped away the disagreement with a wave of his hand. "The point is we learned how to coordinate. Like I'd call Henry when something Navajo came up and find out where he was on it. And Henry'd call me when he had something that was crossing the Checkerboard lines and ask me if we was touchy about it. And if we was touchy, he'd stay over on the reservation and let it alone."

Sena replaced the pencil between his teeth and sat back in the chair. The pencil pointed directly at Chee's nose. Sena's eyes asked Chee if he had received the warning.

"Sounds sensible," Chee said.

"Yeah," Sena said. "It's sensible." He pushed back the swivel chair and pushed himself out of it. "Been a long day," he said. "Get a little dustin' of snow and the goddamn Texans coming through on I-40 ain't never seen it before and we got 'em slid off the road all the way from Gallup to Albuquerque." Sena moved around the desk, agile for such a bulky man, showing Chee out.

"I think you was smart deciding not to take that job," he said. "We'll just solve that little burglary for Mrs. Vines ourself. Just show her how to do it. She say anything about Dillon Charley? Anything at all?"

Again it seemed to Chee that the question was deliberately casual.

"Just what I told you," Chee said.

"You know, they got old Dillon Charley buried up there. Right by the house. That always seemed awful funny to me."

Chee said nothing. Sena's hand gripped his arm.

"She say anything about why they did that?"

"No," Chee said. "All she said was something about the old man joking about it when the doctor told him he was dying."

"About that burglary. You think she was telling all she knew?"

"People usually don't," Chee said.

Sena eyed him thoughtfully. "Yes," he said. "That's always been my experience." He released Chee's elbow. "You be careful, now," he said.

4

JIMMY CHEE SAT with his boot heels propped on the edge of his wastebasket and his fingers locked behind his head and his eyes on Officer Trixie Dodge. Officer Dodge was, as she had already told him, trying to get some work done.

"Come on, Trixie," Chee said. "Think about it. What could be in the box? Why is old lady Vines so hot to get it back? Why is old Gordo Sena so uptight about it?"

Officer Dodge was sorting through legal papers in her in box, transferring them into a cardboard folder. The papers were to be delivered this morning to the Bureau of Indian Affairs office in Gallup. Officer Dodge was running late. "How the hell would I know?" Trixie said.

"And you never heard of anything called the People of Darkness?"

"Nope," Trixie said. "I've heard of moles. I've heard of the peyote church. In fact, I've got a cousin who's into that." Officer Dodge put the last of the papers into the folder and headed for the door. "And I've heard of people with moles, but I never heard of people who call themselves moles."

"Maybe it had something to do with an amulet, or a fetish—something like that," Chee said.

"Of a mole?" Officer Dodge's voice was incredulous. "What kind of a Navajo would use a mole for an amulet?" Officer Dodge left for Gallup without waiting for an answer.

What kind of a Navajo would use a mole for an amulet? It was a fair enough question. Chee sat, feet on wastebasket, hands locked behind head, thinking about it. It wouldn't be a traditional, old-fashioned Navajo, probably, except under unusual circumstances. More likely one of those Eastern Navajos whose clans had mixed more Pueblo Indian ritualism and Christianity into their culture. The Navajo used representations of the predator Holy People for his amulets. The mole was a predator in the Navajo mythology, but he was much less powerful and much less popular than his more glamorous cousins—the bear, the badger, the eagle, the mountain lion, and so forth. In Chee's own medicine pouch, suspended from a thong inside his trousers, was the figure of a badger. It was about the size of Chee's thumb and carved from soapstone, a gift from his father. In the mythology of the Slow Talking Dinee, Hosteen Badger was a formidable figure. Hosteen Mole played a trivial role. Why use the mole? He was the predator of the nadir, downward, one of the six sacred directions. He was the symbol of the dark underground, with access to those strange dark subsurface worlds through which the Dinee rose in their evolution toward human status. But compared to the bear, the eagle, or even the horned frog, he had little power and no prominence in ceremonials. Why pick the mole? The only explanation Chee could think of was the obvious one. The oil well drilled toward the nadir, into the mole's domain.

Chee unlocked his hands and put his feet squarely on the floor beneath his desk. He should get some reports finished. But halfway through the first one he found himself thinking of the nervous Rosemary Vines offering three thousand dollars for a box of keepsakes and the intense, probing questions of Gordo Sena. An arrogant woman presumed he could be bought, and an autocratic man presumed he could be bluffed. What was it that made this little burglary so important to them?

Chee picked up the Albuquerque telephone book. He found the number and placed a call to the Bernalillo County Medical Center. Two transfers later, he was talking to a nurse in the Cancer Research and Treatment Center.

"I'm sorry," she said. "The patient can't have any visitors."

"We're investigating a crime," Chee said. "Mr. Charley is the only one who can provide some information we need. It would be two or three quick questions."

"Mr. Charley is not conscious," she said. "He's under sedation. He's in very critical condition."

"It would only take a few seconds. I could come and wait for him to regain consciousness," Chee said.

"I'm afraid that won't happen," the nurse said. "He's dying."

Chee thought about that. It made the question he was going to ask sound absurd.

"Can the hospital confirm that Emerson Charley didn't leave the hospital last Tuesday?"

"We can confirm that Mr. Charley hasn't left his room for a month. He's being fed intravenously. He's too weak to move." The tone was disapproving.

"Well, then," Chee said, "I'll need the name of his next of kin."

He got it from the records office, and jotted it on his note pad. Tomas Charley, Rural Route 2, Grants. No telephone. A son, grandson of Dillon Charley. What would Tomas know of something that had happened about the time he was born? Probably not much. Perhaps nothing.

Then who would know?

One question, at least, Chee could find an answer for. What had caused the trouble between Sheriff Sena and Henry Becenti? He would locate Becenti and ask him. And then Chee would decide whether he would collect Mrs. Vines' three thousand dollars.

5

SOME OF IT'S EASY to remember," Henry Becenti said. "Hard not to. Six people killed. But hell. It was way back in '47 or '48. That's a long time ago."

"I can just remember hearing somebody talking about it," Chee said. "But it was long before my time."

"It was a little independent outfit," Becenti recalled. "Trying to do some drilling back in there northeast of Mount Taylor, and they had an explosion that wiped out the whole crew. That's how old Gordo and I got in trouble with each other."

"Just an accident?"

"Yeah," Becenti said. "You know anything about oil drilling? Well, this one was a dry hole. No oil. So they was going to shoot it. Perforate the casing." Becenti glanced at Chee to see if he understood. "They lower a tube of nitroglycerin down the well to the level where it looks best and they shoot it off. Idea is to shatter the rocks down there and get the oil running into the hole. Anyway, this time the nitro went off on the floor of the rig. Wiped everybody out. Little pieces of 'em scattered all over."

A look of distaste crossed Becenti's face. He shook his head, shaking off the vividness of the memory. They were sitting on a shelf of stone that jutted from the slope above Henry Becenti's place. They were there because Chee's arrival had coincided with a visit from Becenti's mother-in-law to Becenti's wife. Changing Woman had taught the original Navajo clans that while the groom should join his bride's family, the mother-in-law and son-in-law should scrupulously avoid all contact. In forty years, Old Woman Nez and Henry Becenti had never broken that taboo. Becenti had built his house at his in-laws' place, but away from the hogan of his bride's parents. When Old Woman Nez came to call, Becenti arranged to be elsewhere. This high ridge, which looked across the great valley of Ambrosia Lakes, was a favored retreat.

"If it was an accident, what was bothering Sena?" Chee asked.

"Sena's older brother was one of them," Becenti said. "He was one of the drillers. I think he was what they call the 'tool pusher.' And Sena got sort of crazy about it."

Becenti shook a cigaret out of his pack, offered it to Chee, and then selected one for himself and struck a kitchen match to it. He sat smoking, looking at Mount Taylor, thirty miles to the east. The sun had dropped behind the horizon, but the top of the mountain, rising a mile above the valley floor, still caught the direct light. Tsoodzil, the Navajos called it, the Turquoise Mountain. It was one of the four sacred peaks which First Man had built to guard Dinetah. He had built it on a blue blanket of earth carried up from the underworld, and decorated it with turquoise and blue flint. And then he had pinned it to the earth with a magic knife, and assigned Turquoise Girl to live there and Big Snake to guard her until the Fourth World ended. Now it appeared the magic knife had slipped. The sacred mountain seemed to float in the sky, cut off from the solid earth by the ground haze.

Beautiful, Chee thought. And on the other side of the mountain was the home of B. J. Vines, who had a wife who decided the theft of a keepsake box was very, very important and probably involved witchcraft, or something akin to it. The smoke from Becenti's cigaret reached Chee's nostrils.

"The first couple of days we thought we had twelve people killed," Becenti said. "Wasn't no way of telling. Lot of people around there now, but then there wasn't nobody for miles. The only ones we could find that heard the explosion were a long ways off. They hadn't gone to see about it. Sometimes the crew stayed out on the rig for several days, so nobody got to wondering about it until the weekend. Somebody got nervous. Gordo was a deputy then. He went out to see about it."

Becenti inhaled a lungful of cigaret and exhaled slowly. The smoke made shapes in the motionless air. Seen in profile, his face was ageless. But his eyes had spent more than forty years looking at drunks, at knife fighters, at victims, at what happened when pickup trucks hit culverts at eighty. They were old eyes.

"The blast was on a Friday, I think it was. Gordo got out there Monday. The birds had been there, and the coyotes. Hauling bits and pieces off." He glanced at Chee, making sure he understood the implications. "Anyway, like I said, his brother worked out there. Gordo couldn't find him. Or couldn't find enough to know whether it was his brother or not. And then one of the men that we thought was killed showed up in Grants. It turned out there was a crew of six roustabouts working out there and we had 'em all down as dead and they was all alive."

Becenti's old eyes looked away from the mountain and made contact with Chee's. "They'd been warned not to go to work," he said.

"It was an accident," Chee said slowly. "Who knew it was going to happen?"

"Their foreman was a peyote chief. He'd had services the night before and he had a vision," Becenti said. "God talked to him and God told him something bad was going to happen out at the well."

"And he warned his crew?"

"That's right," Becenti said. "And when Sena found out about it he just about went crazy. Sena didn't believe in visions. He figured there was some funny business and somebody had killed his brother."

"Hard to blame him," Chee said.

"Anyway, Sena had three of the crew locked up at Grants and was looking for the peyote chief. I was, too—for illegal use of a narcotic on the reservation. One of our people found him first and we had him in custody when a deputy sheriff got there to arrest him." Becenti's wrinkled face folded itself into a grin. "Big damned argument over who was gonna get him. Whether it was reservation land or county jurisdiction where he lived, and where the oil well was. Looked like we was going to have another Indian war there for a while. But the well wasn't on Navajo land, so I let Sena have him."

Becenti inhaled a puff of cigaret smoke, breathed it out, and looked at the mountain. Its slopes were rosy now with the sunset. Chee said nothing. In Navajo fashion, when Becenti knew what he wanted to say next he would say it. There was no reason to hurry.

"Nothing ever came of it," Becenti said. "Not as far as Sena was concerned. The peyote preacher stuck to his story, and there wasn't any reason in the world to believe anyone would have blown up those men on purpose, and so finally Sena turned him loose. But something came of it for us. The Council wanted the peyote church stopped. So we was trying to arrest anyone with peyote. But word got around about the preacher saving those lives, and the congregation kept growing."

"And you kept arresting them?"

"Trying to," Becenti said. "They kept moving the

services around. First one place and then another. Sort of went underground." Becenti laughed again. "Got real secret. The leaders took to wearing mole amulets and they called themselves the People of Darkness." Becenti used the same Navajo word that Mrs. Vines had remembered.

"The peyote chief was a Navajo named Dillon Charley?"

"That's right," Becenti said. "He was the peyote chief. He was the one who had the vision."

"Did B. J. Vines have anything to do with that oil well?"

"No," Becenti said. "He didn't come into this country until after all that happened." Becenti slammed his fist into his palm. "By God, though," he said. "Vines and Charley got connected later on. Charley worked for him. After that explosion Sena hated Charley and pretty soon Sena was hating Vines, too." He glanced at Chee. "How much you know about Vines?"

"Just what I've heard," Chee said. "Came in here a poor boy at the very beginning of the uranium discoveries. Made the big uranium find on Section 17 and sold his leases to Anaconda for ten million dollars and a percentage royalty on the ore, and now he gets a little richer every time they drive an ore truck out of the Red Deuce Mine. Got more money than the U.S. government, big-game hunter, flies an airplane, so forth."

"That's about it," Becenti said. "Except early on he and Sena had their troubles. Sena was sheriff by then, and Vines ran some Anglo against him and spent a lot of money and be damned if he didn't beat Sena. And Sena came back two years later and beat the Anglo. Sena's been sheriff of Valencia ever since, and he never did forgive Vines."

"How did Charley get involved with Vines?" Chee asked.

"Politics. He started working with Vines against Sena—getting out the Navajo vote, and the Lagunas and Acomas. On Vines' payroll, probably. Later on he worked out there at Vines' ranch. Died years ago."

"What happened to the People of Darkness?"

"Haven't heard of them for years," Becenti said. "But the church is still operating. You remember the courts ruled that peyote was a sacrament and they had a right to dope themselves up with it. Charley's son—I think his name was Emerson—he was the preacher after Dillon died. And Emerson's boy, he's a peyote chief since Emerson's sick."

"Tomas Charley?"

Becenti nodded. "He's a crazy little son of a bitch," Becenti said. "All them Charleys was crazy and this youngest one is the worst. His mother's a Laguna. From what I hear, he's into one of the Laguna kiva societies, and he's the peyote chief in the Native American Church around here, and he does some curing for the People on top of it all."

"How'd that happen?" Chee asked.

"One of the boy's paternal uncles is a *yataalii*," Becenti said. "Pretty good old fellow. He taught

Tomas the Blessing Way and the kid does it now and then. But most people would rather get someone else."

"Why do you say he's crazy?"

Becenti laughed and shrugged. "Chewed too god-damn many peyote buttons," he said. "Got his brains curdled. Sees visions. Thinks he's talking to God. Silly little bastard." Becenti paused, searching for an illustration. "He come in the office last year and said Jesus had told him there was going to be a terrible drought and we should warn everybody to stock up on food. And then this fall he was in telling us that some witch was making his daddy sick. His daddy, that's Emerson Charley."

"Well, it's been dry as hell," Chee said, "and his daddy is dying."

"It's always dry," Becenti said. "And his daddy's got cancer. That's what I heard. I didn't know he was dying." Becenti thought about it. "Anyway, he didn't get witched. I think cancer runs in that family, like craziness. I think that's what the grandfather died of, too."

"Dillon Charley? Yeah. That's what Mrs. Vines said."

Becenti looked uneasy. He was old enough to have the traditions of the People worn deep into the grain, and one of the traditions was not to speak the name of the dead. The ghost might overhear and be summoned to the speaker.

"Did you know Vines had Dillon Charley buried up at his house?" Chee asked.

"I heard that," Becenti said. "White men sure got some weird customs."

Especially their burial customs, Chee thought. He'd spent years among the whites, first at boarding school, then through enough years at the University of New Mexico to win a degree in anthropology, but he still couldn't fathom the attitude of whites toward the corpse.

"You have any idea why Vines would want to bury Dillon Charley?" Chee asked.

Becenti made a wry face. "Hell, no."

"This Tomas Charley," Chee said. "You said he was crazy. Would he be crazy enough to get into Vines' house and steal a lockbox with keepsakes in it?"

Becenti extracted the cigaret from between his lips and looked at Chee. "Did something like that happen?" he asked. "Why would he want to steal something like that? Vines and his woman are both big hunters. I understand either one of them would just as soon shoot somebody as not."

"I heard that Tomas' grandfather thought Vines kept the luck of the Darkness People in that box," Chee said. "Maybe Tomas heard about that."

Becenti nodded. "Okay, then. I'd say yes. That kid would be about crazy enough to break in to steal himself some luck."

6

THE SPIKE on his desk the next morning held three pink "While You Were Out" slips. One told him to call Captain Leaphorn at the Chinle substation. The other two, one left over from yesterday, and one received just before he'd got to work, told him to call B. J. Vines. He put those aside and called the Chinle station. Leaphorn's business involved identifying a middle-aged Navajo killed in a truck-pedestrian accident. The captain wanted him to send someone to Thoreau to check with a family there. Chee added it to the afternoon assignment of Officer Dodge. Then he picked up the "Call B. J. Vines" slips, leaned back in his chair and considered them. Both were initialed "T.D." Trixie Dodge was at her desk across the room. He glanced at her. She looked grim this morning. Trixie, he suspected, should have written "Call Mrs. B. J. Vines." Vines wouldn't be back for weeks.

"Hey, Trixie," he said. "You put down 'Call Vines' here. Wasn't the call from Mrs. Vines?"

Trixie didn't look up. "Vines," she said.

"*Mr.* Vines?" Chee insisted.

"It was a man. He said his name was B. J. Vines. He asked for you and then he asked you to call him at that number." Trixie's voice was patient.

Chee dialed the number. It rang once.

"Yes." The voice was male.

"This is Jim Chee of the Navajo Tribal Police. I have a note to call B. J. Vines."

"Oh, good," the voice said. "I'm Vines. I'd like to talk to you about that little theft we had. Could you come out?"

"When?"

"Well," the voice said, "the sooner the better. I understand my wife talked to you about it and . . ." The voice paused and interjected a nervous laugh. "Well, there's some misunderstandings that need to be cleared up." The tone was ironic now. "There tends to be when Rosemary gets involved."

"Okay," Chee said. "I'll be out there after lunch."

"Good," Vines said. "Thanks."

Chee marked the Thoreau assignment off Dodge's assignment sheet. It was on his way. He'd handle it himself.

7

THE PUEBLO WOMAN ANSWERED the door-
bell and showed Chee into the predator room without a sign she'd ever seen him before. There was a
man behind the glass-topped desk now—a small man
with a round face made rounder by the great bush of
iron-gray beard that surrounded it. The man pulled
himself to his feet. "Ben Vines," he said, offering a
small, hard hand. "Have a seat." Chee sat. So did
Vines. The room was brighter now than it had been
when he had seen it with Mrs. Vines. Autumn sunlight streamed in, reflecting from the glass eyeballs
and ivory teeth of the cats. The sunlight made the
room less hostile. The lioness above Vines' left shoulder seemed to be smiling. So did Vines.

"I understand my wife told you we had a break-in,
and she hired you to solve the crime," Vines said.

"She asked me," Chee said.

"This is embarrassing," Vines said. What Chee
could see of his face through its frame of hair didn't
look embarrassed. His alert black eyes were study-

ing Chee. "I have a feeling there really isn't a crime to be solved."

"No?"

"No," Vines said. He laughed. "My wife is not a very predictable woman at times. She's a very nervous woman. Sometimes things get confused."

"Having someone break into your wall safe can make you nervous," Chee said.

"How nervous it makes you depends on who broke into it," Vines said. He shifted his weight, glanced out the window and then back at Chee. "Do you know where the safe is?"

"It's behind that head," Chee said, nodding to the appropriate cat.

Vines got to his feet again and maneuvered himself laboriously to the wall. He balanced carefully and lifted the mounted head off its hook, dumping it on the carpet. The safe door eased itself open on well-oiled hinges. The space behind it was dark and empty. Vines looked at it, his expression thoughtful. He extracted a pack of cigarets from the side pocket of his jacket, shook one out and lit it. At his feet, the cat's head smiled benignly at the ceiling.

"Rosemary and I weren't young when we married," Vines said. "We'd enjoyed lives of our own and we were going to continue to be private persons as well as man and wife. We kept our old friends and our old memories. Both of us. Separate."

Vines had been talking to the safe. Now he glanced around at Chee. A trickle of tobacco smoke leaked through his lips. It made its way through his mustache like gray fog. Chee could see now that the left side of Vines' face was affected. The corner of his mouth and the muscles around his left eye drooped. "This safe operates with a key and a combination. Rosemary doesn't have either one of them. I have a toolbox in the stables. There's a prying bar in it." Vines pushed the safe door closed. "You'll notice that this wall safe is like a lot of wall safes. It has a limited purpose and it's not built like a bank vault. It's not designed to do more than slow down a safe-cracker. You can take a pry bar and jam it in the door fitting, and it gives you enough leverage to spring the lock. Take a look."

Chee looked. He noticed, as he'd noticed the first time he'd examined it, that the safe door did seem to have been pried open. Whatever had been used had left marks, and the door had been slightly bent. Once again, that seemed odd. The door was heavy. Unless it was poor metal, it would take tremendous strength to bend it even with the leverage of a wrecking bar. Chee looked for a trademark and found none.

"I think you should get your money back on that door," he said.

Vines laughed. "I'm afraid the warranty's run out. As a matter of fact, I had the safe made and installed, and I guess they didn't use the most expensive material."

"Who did it for you?"

"I don't remember," Vines said. "Some outfit in Albuquerque. I had it done when I built this place, and that was thirty years ago." He pushed the door shut. "The point I was making was that Rosemary doesn't have a key to the wall safe, but she does have a key to the tool locker. The pry bar was gone. I found it in her closet."

"Oh," Chee said.

Vines shrugged. He produced a wry face. "So I want to apologize for all this. And I'd like to pay you for your trouble." He produced a check. "You made two trips out here. Would two hundred dollars be fair?"

Chee glanced from Vines to the sly smile of the tiger. He thought of the bent metal of the door and the empty space behind the door, and of what Mrs. Vines had told him. Among other things, she had told him that B. J. Vines was away at a hospital. But two hundred dollars was too much to be offered. Vines was watching him. Vines had told him, in effect, that the crime was family business, and thus no crime at all, and no concern of Chee's. To ask a question now would be impertinent.

"Did Mrs. Vines have the box?" Chee asked.

Vines considered this impertinence, his mild eyes on Chee's face. He sighed. "I don't know," he said. "Maybe she had it. Maybe she disposed of it. The point is it doesn't matter. I think she told you there wasn't much in it. There wasn't. Mementos. Things that reminded me of the past. Nothing of value. Not even to me any longer."

Vines held the check toward Chee, dangling it between his fingers.

"I understand you reported it to the sheriff," he

said. "Of course you'd have to do that. Old Gordo came out yesterday to ask about it. I wondered how much you told him."

"Just what Mrs. Vines told me."

Vines took three careful steps toward Chee and put the check in Chee's shirt pocket.

"This isn't necessary," Chee said. "I'm not even sure it's allowed."

"Take it," Vines said. "Rosemary and I will both feel better. If it's against policy, tear it up. I wonder if you noticed that our sheriff is very interested in my business?" Vines made his laborious way back to his chair.

"I noticed," Chee said.

"Did he ask a lot of questions?"

"Yep," Chee said. Vines waited for more. He realized gradually that it wouldn't be forthcoming.

"Gordo asked me a lot of questions about the People of Darkness," Vines said. "I got the impression that you'd told him Rosemary thought one of the Charley boys had taken the box."

"That's right," Chee said.

Vines waited again. He sighed. "I've had a lot of trouble with Gordo Sena," he said. "Years ago. I thought it was over with." Vines put out his cigaret and walked to the window. Past him, Chee could see an expanse of Mount Taylor's east slope. At this altitude it was the zone of transition from ponderosa pine into fir, spruce, and aspen. The ground under the aspens was yellow with fallen leaves. The slanting sunlight created a golden glow a little like fire.

"It was early in the 1950s," Vines said. "I'd found that uranium deposit that the Red Deuce is mining now, and I was building this place, and I hired a Navajo named Dillon Charley as a sort of foreman to look after things. I didn't know it, but Gordo had a thing about Charley, and about a bunch of other Indians in a church old Dillon was running." Vines glanced back at Chee, the window light giving his gray beard a translucent frosting. "It was the peyote church. It was against tribal law in those days."

"I know about it," Chee said.

"Well, Sena was dogging them. He was picking them up, and beating them up. I got involved in it. Hired a lawyer over in Grants to take care of bonding them out and to bitch to the Justice Department about rights violations, and finally I put up some money behind a candidate and we got Sena beat for reelection for one term. For several years there, it was hairy between Sena and me. Things had settled down for the last few years. I'm wondering if he wants to stir it up again. That's why I wanted to know what kind of questions he was asking you."

"He asked why your wife wanted to hire me," Chee said. He gave Vines a quick résumé of Sena's questions.

"What do you think of that oil well business?" Vines asked. "Did Sena tell you about that? About why he hated old Dillon Charley?"

"He didn't talk about it," Chee said. "But I understand he thinks it's funny Dillon Charley got that advance warning."

"You don't believe in visions?" Through the bristling whiskers Vines' expression seemed to be amused. Chee couldn't be sure.

"It depends," Chee said. "But I don't believe in crimes without motives. No one can find one for this explosion, I guess."

"Well, there are some theories."

"Like what?"

"You know Sena's, I guess. He doesn't seem to have any ideas about a motive, but he appears to think that Dillon Charley was tied up in some sort of conspiracy. And then there's another theory that Gordo did it himself."

"Why?"

"The way the story goes, the older brother was the apple of everybody's eye—including his mother's. Gordo is supposed to have known that the old lady was leaving the ranch to Robert. So he blows up the oil well."

"How'd he handle it?"

Vines shrugged. "I don't know," he said. "I heard it was a nitroglycerin explosion, some sort of charge they lower down into the shaft of oil wells to shake things up, but it went off too early. I guess you could set that stuff off by shooting into it with a rifle. It was all before my time."

"How does the Sena-did-it theory explain Dillon Charley's vision?"

"That's easy," Vines said. "Dillon finds out somehow that Sena was planning something funny. So he arranges to have his peyote vision at the church service, and he tells his crew to stay away from the well. Sena blows the place up, but he finds out that Dillon must have known something. So he tries to drive him away with the harassment."

"Could be," Chee said.

"I think Gordo would like to know if Dillon Charley told me anything," Vines said. "Did his questions lead that way?"

"More or less," Chee said. "Did Dillon Charley tell you anything?"

Vines smiled. "Did Gordo tell you to ask me that?"

"You brought it up," Chee said. "I'll change the question. What do you think happened out at that oil well?"

"I understand nitro is touchy stuff. In those days those accidents happened. I think they had another case like that in the state a few years earlier."

"Do you think it was an accident? Do you think Dillon Charley was just nervous about having the nitro at the well?"

Vines swiveled his chair to give himself a view out the window. Chee could see only his profile.

"I think Gordo Sena murdered his brother," Vines said.

8

COLTON WOLF WAS RUNNING a little be-
hind schedule. He had prepared *oeufs en gelée* for his
breakfast. He meticulously followed the recipe in
Gourmet and that took time. The aspic required
twelve minutes at a rolling boil, and preparing the
purée of peas for the garnish took longer still, and
then another hour was required to allow the eggs to
cool properly in their molds of aspic. It was midmorning when he folded away the breakfast linen
and cleared the silver and china from the Formica
top of his trailer's eating surface. He had planned to
work two hours on the model Baldwin steam engine
he was building. Now he cut that to eighty minutes,
working most of the time with his jeweler's glass in
his eye and getting much of the fitting done on the
piston assembly. The alarm dinged at 11:35 A.M. Colton pulled the covers over his lathe and drill and put
his metal working tools carefully back in their
proper places in his toolbox and the toolbox back in
his lock cabinet. The cabinet also held his collection

of steam engines, all of which actually operated—blowing whistles, driving belts, and turning wheels—and all of which had been made by Colton himself. The engines sat among the tools of his trade—two rifles, the chambers and trigger assembly sections of three pistols, an assortment of barrels to be screwed into these assemblies, an array of silencers, three small boxes trailing insulated wires, which were bomb detonaters, a candy box which held plastic explosive (Colton kept eight sticks of dynamite and his dynamite caps safely cool in the refrigerator), and a row of cans of shaving cream and spray deodorant. Except for the rifles and their telescopic sights, he had manufactured much of this paraphernalia himself—partly because if it wasn't purchased it couldn't be traced and partly because some of it couldn't be bought. The shaving cream and deodorant cans were Colton's way of getting his tools through the x-ray stations at airport loading gates. One could fit the parts of one of Colton's pistols plus its silencer into two cans, screw the tops back on, and show an airport inspection nothing more questionable than Burma Shave. The bomb detonators were also the products of Colton's skill. He'd learned the principle from a former Special Services soldier he'd met in Idaho's Point-of-the-Mountain prison. It involved two batteries and a little ball of mercury which closed the electrical connection when the box moved.

Colton locked it all away, and went to make his mail check.

It wasn't that Colton Wolf expected any mail. It was part of the routine by which he lived. In whatever town he parked his trailer, Colton immediately rented a post office box. He rented it in the name of whatever commercial-sounding noun came to mind. Then he mailed a note to Boxholder at a post office box number in El Paso, Texas, in which he reported his new address. That was Colton's link to the man who provided him with his assignments. It was his only link with the world. In Colton Wolf's mind, and sometimes in his dreams, it was the flaw through which the world would someday catch him and kill him. Colton wished there were another way to do business. There wasn't. So he minimized the risk as much as he could. Minimizing risks was very much a part of Colton Wolf's life.

He drove his GMC pickup slowly past the branch post office, inspecting parked cars. Nothing looked suspicious. He parked at the Safeway lot and strolled the block and a half to the post office, taking inventory of what he saw. Two women and a man were in the lobby. The clerks behind the counter were familiar faces. Colton walked to the wall of post office boxes. Through the glass of box 1191 he could see an envelope. He ignored it and inspected box 960. It was empty. Colton walked out through the lobby, memorizing the customers. He went back to the Safeway, bought a small filet, a half pound of mushrooms, a pound of white grapes, a half pint of cream, and an ounce of black pepper. He put the groceries in the truck, climbed in himself, and tuned in a country western music station on the radio. He let twenty minutes pass while he listened. Then he walked back to the post office. Five customers were in the lobby now and none matched the previous three. Colton walked directly to box 1191 and removed the envelope. A smaller envelope lay under it. He slipped both into his jacket pocket and returned to the truck. No one followed him, and no one followed him a few minutes later as he drove back up the freeway ramp. Colton Wolf had survived another contact with the world.

The smaller envelope was addressed simply to his box number. It contained a slip of paper on which a series of numerals was penciled. Properly sorted out, they gave Colton a telephone number to call and the time of 2:10 P.M. to call it. He had put the slip in his shirt pocket. The second envelope bore the return address of Webster Investigations and a Los Angeles street number. Colton had known that it would, since no one else knew his box number, but even so he had felt his stomach tighten as he put the envelope on the seat beside him. When he got home he would open it. Meanwhile he would try not to think about it.

In the trailer, he put away the groceries and plugged in the coffeepot. Then he sat in his recliner, dried his palms on his trouser legs, slit open the envelope, and removed the contents. Two typewritten pages were folded around an expense statement. Wolf put the statement aside.

Dear Mr. Wolf:

First the bad news, which is that the lead I had run across in Anaheim didn't pay off. The woman was far too young to be your mother. I found her birth certificate in the county courthouse before I made arrangements with the detective in Anaheim, so I saved you that money.

The good news is that I located a truckdriver who worked at the Mayflower agency in Bakersfield in the early 1960s and he remembers working with Buddy Shaw. He found an address where Shaw lived in San Francisco. It's old, but it will give us a place to start tracking him down. . . .

Wolf finished the first page, laid it carefully on the arm of the recliner, and read through the second page. That done, he read both pages again, very slowly. Then he glanced at the itemized statement. It covered a month, charging Wolf for five days of time and an assortment of expenses which added up to a little more than eleven hundred dollars. He sat then with his slender, long-fingered hands resting in his lap, and thought.

His face, too, was slender, and his body and his bones, but a sinewy tension about him gave his thinness the look of a honed blade. His hair was thin, the shade of old straw, and his eyebrows and lashes were almost invisible against pale, freckled skin. His eyes were a faint blue-green—about the tint of old ice. Colton Wolf looked bleached, drained of pigment, antiseptic, neat, emotionless.

In fact, at the moment his emotions were mixed. At one level of his intelligence, Colton was encouraged. The detective would find Buddy Shaw. Shaw would still be living with Colton's mother. Or Shaw would know where to find her. And then there would be the reunion. At another level, Colton believed none of that. Webster was screwing him. The private detective had been screwing him for four expensive years. There were no trips, no hotel bills, no long-distance calls, no trace of Buddy Shaw. Webster had had no more success than the first private detective Colton had hired. Webster simply sat in his office in Encino and once a month dreamed up a letter and fabricated an itemized bill. The first detective had gone to the house Colton and his mother and Buddy Shaw had occupied in Bakersfield. He had found it occupied by transients who knew absolutely nothing helpful. Absolutely nothing about a man and a woman and a child who had lived there nineteen years before. Colton had destroyed that report, tearing it savagely into shreds. But he still remembered what it said. It said the house was now occupied by a Mexican woman. The realtor who handled the place kept records back only five years. During that time there had been three other occupants. None had left forwarding addresses. There was no record in the county courthouse of a marriage between a man named Buddy Shaw, or any other Shaw, and a woman named Linda Betty Fry. Mayflower Van Lines records showed that a Buddy Shaw had been employed at their warehouse for eleven months nineteen years earlier. He had been fired for drunk-enness. Police records showed an E. W. Shaw, a.k.a. Buddy Shaw, three times. He had been booked once for drunk and disorderly, had done thirty days for aggravated assault, and had been arrested for assault with a deadly weapon. No disposition of that was recorded. Relative to the woman herself there was hardly a trace. Just the booking sheet on Shaw, showing a woman identified as Linda Betty Maddox, brought in with him on the disorderly charge.

Colton remembered the letter in detail. He especially remembered the final paragraph:

Unless you can provide more information relative to this woman, there's no hope of finding her. Can you tell us her age, where she was born, something about her family, mother, father, brothers, sisters, where she was educated, where she was married, or any information about her past? Without such information to develop leads, there is simply no hope of finding her.

No hope of finding her. He had been living in Oklahoma City then, using the name Fry. He had driven to Bakersfield. Two hard days and nights on the highway. In Nevada, he'd decided his name probably wasn't Fry. Maybe it was Maddox, but it wasn't Fry. He remembered Fry faintly—a round, dark, pock-marked face, a round belly, a sullen, unhappy mouth. They had lived with him in San Jose and Colton had been Colton Fry in school there. He'd assumed Fry was his father. Perhaps it was someone named Maddox. Colton could remember no one by that name. Somewhere west of Las Vegas, he'd decided to choose a neutral name for himself. He'd use it only until he could find his mother. She'd tell him his real name. She'd tell him about his father, and his grandparents. And about the family home. It would be in a small town, Colton thought, and there'd be a graveyard with tombstones for the family. When he found her, she'd tell him who he was. Until then, he'd pick a last name. Something simple. He picked Wolf.

The coffee was perking now on the butane burner. Through the aluminum walls of the trailer came the sound of a truck's air horn blaring on the freeway. Colton was not conscious of either sound. He was remembering arriving in Bakersfield, the drive to the old neighborhood. The Mexican woman who came to the door spoke no English, but her daughter had talked to him. She knew nothing of a thin, blue-eyed blond woman named Linda Betty, nor of a burly man named Buddy Shaw. He could see the girl now, nervous at his questioning. And he could see the cracked concrete steps as he left the porch—no more broken now than they had been when he was eleven and had sat on them those nights when Buddy Shaw and his mother were drunk, had sat waiting for Shaw to go to sleep so that he could slip in.

Colton had stood beside his pickup, looking back at the house. The sparse grass he remembered was no longer there, the glass in one window was replaced by plywood. But otherwise it looked much the same. The last time he had seen it was the day after his twelfth birthday—the last time he had come home. The boy he knew at school had said he couldn't stay at his house any longer and he had walked home to see if Buddy Shaw had sobered up, and if Buddy Shaw would let him return. He had found the house empty. He had peered through the windows and seen the kitchen stripped of his mother's pans, and the bathroom stripped of her toiletries. But in the room where he slept, his things were still scattered. The bedclothing was gone from the cot, but the blue jacket his mother had got for him somewhere was still hanging on its peg. And his books were there. And his cap. He had broken a window and gone inside, cutting his hand in his panic. There had been nothing except the old furniture that had been there when they moved in and his own spare clothing.

Colton Wolf stirred uneasily in the recliner. All the desolation of that discovery came back to him again—the sense of loss and confusion and rejection, and with it the bleak, hopeless loneliness. Where could she be? How could he find her? Why had she gone? On the burner, the percolator gave a final cough and fell silent, its duty done. Colton Wolf ignored the sound, if he heard it. He was considering the same questions he'd considered for nineteen years.

A few minutes after one-thirty, he pushed himself out of the recliner and poured a cup of coffee. He took it to the truck, to sip as he drove. At a pay booth beside Central Avenue he made the call. He dialed the El Paso, Texas, area code, and the prefix number, and then waited while the second hand of his watch swept toward 2:10. Then he completed the dialing. He dropped in the coins and heard the number ring just a moment before the second hand swept past his deadline.

It was answered instantly. "This is Boxholder," the voice said. That address had become something of a joke between them. A joke and a code.

"Okay," Colton said. "Boxholder here, too."

"We have another opportunity in New Mexico," the voice said. "One thing led to another, I guess."

"Same client?" Colton asked.

Silence. "We never talk about clients," Boxholder said. "Remember?"

"Sorry," Colton said.

"Conditions are a lot the same, though. The subject won't be on guard. And there's a hurry."

"How much hurry?" Colton asked. Hurry bothered him. And his voice showed it.

"Nothing specific," Boxholder said. "Just the quicker the better. Every day increases the risk. So forth."

"I don't like to rush things," Colton said. "Things go wrong."

"You don't have to handle it," Boxholder said. "Maybe you'd better not. But I know you wanted to clean up that original business, and that kept you in Albuquerque anyway, and . . ."

"I think I'll have the other business finished in twenty-four hours or so," Colton said. "Maybe tonight."

"Well, that's all we're committed to. After that's done we've kept the original contract." Boxholder chuckled. "Took a little longer than anybody figured, but what the hell?" Silence. "I thought maybe you'd like to show these folks how good you usually are."

Colton grimaced. Boxholder assumed the thought of a dissatisfied customer would bother him. That was correct. Boxholder assumed he took intense pride in his work. That was also correct. "Okay," he said. "Tell me about it."

Boxholder told him. Then, as they always did, they arranged the time and telephone number for Colton's report.

Colton used up three hours. He walked. He dropped the letter he had written to Webster Investigations into a mailbox. It contained his check for $1,087.50 and a note suggesting that Webster run personal ads in West Coast newspapers asking Linda Betty Shaw/Fry/Maddox to contact him. He walked some more. He sat on the bench at a bus stop. The bus stop was near a school crossing and he studied the homeward-bound students. They seemed to be junior-high age and younger, and most of them walked in little clusters and bunches, talking. Once a single kid came along, all by herself. Colton guessed the single was somebody who had just moved to the neighborhood. If you did that, you couldn't make friends, because everybody already had them. When he was eight they had lived in San Diego in this one apartment almost a year and he had made a friend there. And then when he was fourteen and had been in Taylorville long enough, he had made a friend or two. But that was different. In reform school nobody knew anybody at first and everybody was looking for connections. Taylorville had been a pretty good place, all in all, and he'd been glad enough to go back for his second stretch. They kept the gays off of you in Taylorville. Not like in Folsom, where he'd done his armed robbery time.

Finally it was late enough. He called the University of New Mexico Hospital and asked for Mrs. Myers on the terminal ward. As always, her voice was placid. "I'm afraid it's all over," she said. "He's been in a coma all day and his heart finally quit."

"Well, you just have to be philosophical about it."

"That's right," Mrs. Myers said. "But it's always a blow."

"Well," Colton said. He found himself searching for something else to say—a way to extend the conversation. But there was no reason for that. He was finished with Mrs. Myers. This would be the last of more than two months of intermittent conversations, all carefully planned, all carefully executed. First he had learned the name of the nurse who ran the middle shift on the cancer ward. He had got that from hospital information by pretending he wanted to send her a thank-you card. And then, on his first call to learn the patient's condition, he had said, "By the way, are you Mrs. Myers? He's told me how kind

you've been to him. I want to thank you for that."
That had set the tone. Colton rarely talked to anyone, but he knew how to do it well. He watched
television, and he listened carefully to conversations
in airports and restaurants and the waiting lines for
movies—the places where people talked to each
other. Once in a while he practiced, with cabdrivers
or the call girls he took to motels twice a month. But
he rarely talked to the same person more than once
or twice, except for Boxholder. After all this time,
he found himself imagining how Mrs. Myers looked
and what she was like—just as he wondered about
Boxholder. He had been tempted to go to the ward
some evening and take a look at her. But that involved a risk. Colton did not take risks. "Well," he
said again. "Thank you very much," and he hung up.

9

COLTON LEFT THE TRAILER just as the ten o'clock news was beginning on Channel 7. He was wearing charcoal slacks, a black pullover, and his crepe-soled shoes. He preferred going bareheaded, but tonight he pulled a navy-blue stocking cap over his straw-colored hair. He took with him a canvas flight bag in which he had put a folding shovel, a green blanket, a white cotton coat with the legend STRONG-THORNE MORTUARY printed on the back, and a New Mexico automobile license plate. He had driven past the Albuquerque airport after telephoning and had collected the plate from a car left in the low-rate parking lot where long-term travelers parked their cars. Then he'd replaced the plate he would use with one switched from another car. If the theft was reported, the police would have the wrong number.

He drove back to the airport now, left his pickup in the upper lot, and rented a Chevrolet station wagon from Hertz, using a driver's license and credit card that identified him as Charles Minton, with a Dallas post office box address. Then he took Interstate 25 south and turned the wagon westward at the Rio Bravo exit. He drove slowly, counting the tenths of miles on the odometer. Near the river, he turned off the pavement onto a narrow dirt road. He got out of the wagon there, taped down the switch to keep the courtesy light off when the door was opened, and replaced the Hertz license with the stolen plates. It was after 11:00 P.M. now, a cloudless night lit by a partial moon. The dirt road crossed a cattle guard, curved across a culvert, and branched. Colton angled left. The road became two tire tracks winding through the cottonwood of the Rio Grande's silted flood plain. The tracks crossed an irrigation drain on a rattling plank bridge and dropped abruptly downward. A hundred jolting yards beyond the drain levee, Colton stopped. His headlights illuminated the stripped body of an old Ford sedan, rusty and riddled with bullet holes. Beyond it was the ruins of another car, also the target of years of hunters. Trash was everywhere—a rotting mattress, the corpse of a refrigerator, cans, bottles, boxes, papers, rags, tattered roofing paper, brush. Colton flicked off headlights and engine and rolled down the windows on both sides of the car. He sat without moving for perhaps ten minutes. He heard the ticking of the cooling engine, and the occasional sound of diesels moving on the interstate far up the valley. It was a windless night and he heard nothing else. Satisfied, he removed the shovel from the bag and climbed out of the wagon.

He pulled the mattress aside and dug where it had been, piling the earth carefully. Even in the dark, it was easy going in the loamy soil. He wanted a hole about six feet long and at least four feet deep.

10

COLTON REACHED the University of New
Mexico parking lot a little before 2 A.M. He had
scouted it before, but two weeks had passed. If anything had changed, Colton wanted to know it early.
He replaced his windbreaker with the mortuary
coat. The woman at the desk didn't look up and the
hall to the elevators was empty. The second-floor
hall was also deserted. So far, fine. But down the hall
Colton could see a paper sign taped to the door of the
morphology laboratory. It read: MORPHOLOGY LABO-
RATORY MOVED TO STATE LABORATORY BUILDING. He
stared at the sign, dismayed. He moved quickly
around the corner. The wide door that opened into
the morgue was still shielded with a sheet of plywood
to protect it from the bumps of metal body carts. He
tried the knob. Locked. He had expected it to be
locked. Would they have moved the morgue along
with the autopsy laboratory? Even if they did, the
hospital would need a place to hold bodies overnight.
From his trouser cuff he extracted a thin steel blade
which he had stitched into place. It proved as quick

as a key. He swung the door shut behind him and found the switch in the darkness. Three body carts were lined against the wall. All were empty. Beyond them the stainless-steel door of the walk-in refrigerator stood closed. Colton swung it open. Two carts were parked inside, each bearing a sheet-shrouded figure. Colton read the tag on the nearest one. It identified the victim as Randy A. Johnson, 23 years old, Roswell, New Mexico. Dead on arrival. Head and neck injuries. Motorcycle accident. Colton checked the next tag. It said: EMERSON CHARLEY. AUTOPSY. HOLD FOR CRTC. "CRTC" would mean Cancer Research and Treatment Center. Colton folded back the sheet. He had seen the face before only at a distance. It was gaunt now, drawn with the effects of a lingering death. But he recognized it. This time nothing would go wrong. He replaced the sheet.

In the hall, he stood a moment, listening. A faint thumping came from the hospital laundry. All else was quiet. Colton glanced at his watch. Five after three. He decided not to wait. The odds, he decided, wouldn't improve.

It was fourteen after three when he parked the station wagon beside the loading dock. The dock door stood partly open, as he had left it, and he could still hear a thumping from the laundry. He left the station wagon's tailgate open. It was thirty-five steps from the doorway of the dock to the morgue door. He picked the lock again and slipped in.

There were two red plastic sacks of clothing on the floor beside the carts. He put the nearest one under the sheet beside the corpse and wheeled the cart out of the refrigerator. At the door of the morgue he paused again, listening. Thirty-five steps, and then perhaps sixty seconds on the dock while he lifted the body into the station wagon. The hall was absolutely silent. The cart rolled down it, trailing the slight sound of rubber tires on tile. On the dock, Colton pushed the cart out of sight of the doorway. He extracted the clothing sack and tossed it into the back of the wagon.

"Come on, friend," he said, and he tucked the sheet around the body and lifted it in his arms. It was stiff with rigor mortis. Surprisingly light. "Here we go now," Colton said. He slid the body into the station wagon and covered it with the green blanket.

The period of high risk was almost over now. He closed the tailgate, rolled the body cart back into the hallway. The station wagon's engine started instantly. As he did the left turn out of the service drive, he glanced in the rear-view mirror. The dock was deserted. No one had seen him. It had gone perfectly. Absolutely no tracks had been left.

Colton tuned in a country western station on his way back to the grave. He felt happier than he had for months. Happy for the first time since he had called Boxholder and told him of the failure. The memory was vivid. Two hours sitting in the airport, waiting for the time to call the El Paso number. Dreading it. He had never failed before. From the very first—torching the nightclub in Denver seven years before—he had always reported only success. Not just success but perfection. The job done. No witnesses. No evidence. No tracks. Perfection. And always Boxholder's voice, warm and friendly, congratulating him. This time there had been no congratulations. First there had been only silence, and then Boxholder's voice was cold.

"Give me the number you're calling from. Wait right there. I'll call the client and call you back. Be there."

"Tell him I won't accept the fee," Colton had said. "Tell him I'll finish the job."

"You just wait," Boxholder said.

Colton had waited. It was more than four hours before the telephone rang.

"Your man was checking into the hospital." Boxholder said. "He's in now. We're to just keep an eye on things and when he dies, you get rid of the body. Get it right away and get rid of it."

"My God," Colton said. "I baby-sit this guy until he dies?"

"Not long," Boxholder said. "He's got a kind of cancer that works fast."

"Then why . . ." Colton let the question trail off.

"Maybe it doesn't work fast enough," Boxholder said. "Do you care?"

"No," Colton said. "I guess not."

But it seemed curious then, and it seemed curious now, this business of getting rid of the body. Curious, but well done. The grave filled. The rotting mattress pulled across it and the trash scattered over the mattress. No one would ever find the body of Emerson Charley. Reporting time was noon tomorrow. Colton anticipated it happily. Boxholder would be pleased.

11

JIM CHEE HAD ROLLED the two-hundred-dollar check from Ben Vines and the five one-hundred-dollar bills from the envelope Mrs. Vines had handed him into a tight cylinder. It was not much larger than a cigaret. Each night he dropped the tube into one of the boots beside his bed. Each morning, after he'd said his brief prayer of greeting to the dawning day, he shook the tube out of the boot and considered what to do with it. And each morning he finally stuck the tube back into his shirt pocket, thereby signaling that the matter remained undecided. On the fourth morning, Chee noticed that the edge of the check was frayed. He unrolled the tube, put check and cash side by side on his table, and stared at them.

Two hundred dollars was too much to be offered for the little trouble he'd been involved in. Worse, why would Mrs. Vines offer him three thousand dollars to recover a box she had stolen herself? For those as inconceivably rich as the Vineses the money would be relatively meaningless. But his uncle had warned him against that kind of thinking.

"Don't think a man don't care about one goat because he's got a thousand of 'em," Hosteen Nakai would say. "He's got a thousand because he cares more about goats than he cares about his relatives." In other words, don't expect the rich to be generous.

And what would his uncle advise him to do about this particular money? Chee grinned, thinking about it. There'd be no advice—not directly. There'd be a hundred questions: Which one was lying? What motivated the large payments? Why did the Checkerboard Navajos think Vines was a witch? Or did they? How was the Charley outfit mixed into this affair? And when Chee could offer no answers, Hosteen Nakai would smile at him and remind him of what he had told Chee a long time ago. He'd told Chee he had to understand white people.

Chee used his two forefingers to tap the stack of currency into a neat pile. Mrs. Vines had lied to him, at least a little. He picked up the check and looked at B. J. Vines' bold signature. Vines' story had been almost purely lies. Chee folded the check and slid it into the credit card pocket of his billfold. He put the currency in the cash compartment. He would talk to Tomas Charley and see what he could learn.

Talking to Tomas Charley meant finding him. Becenti had remembered only that he lived somewhere beyond the eastern limits of the Checkerboard—somewhere near Mount Taylor. Chee made telephone calls. Shortly before noon he learned that

Charley was employed by Kerrmac Nuclear Fuels. A quick call to the Kerrmac personnel office at Grants revealed that Charley was the driver of an ore loader, that he had the day off, that he had no telephone, the rural route address from the Grants' post office matched the one the hospital had provided—a mailbox on the road between Grants and San Mateo village.

It was probably no more than thirty miles from Crownpoint as the raven flew, but for something with wheels it was around ninety. Chee told Officer Benny Yazzie, who was holding down the office, that he wouldn't be back until evening.

While he drove, Chee worked at memorizing the Night Chant. He switched on the tape recorder and ran the cassette forward to the place where the singer awakens the spirit of Talking God in the sacred mask. On Interstate 40, he drove in the slow lane, listening carefully. Truckers, wise to the ways of this stretch of highway, roared past him, safe in the knowledge that tribal police had no jurisdiction here. Passenger cars slowed to the legal fifty-five, eyeing him nervously. Chee ignored them all. He concentrated on the voice of his uncle, strong and sure, singing the words that Changing Woman had taught at the very creation of his people.

> *Above the hills of evening, he stirs, he stirs.*
> *Covered with the pollen of evening, he stirs,*
> *   he stirs.*
> *The Talking God stirs, he stirs amid the sunset.*

Along the trail of beauty, he stirs, he stirs.
With beauty all around him, he stirs, he stirs.

The recorder was on the seat beside him. Chee
silenced Hosteen Nakai's voice with a touch of the off
button, concentrated a moment, then repeated the
five statements, trying to reproduce cadence and
notes as well as meaning. By the time he reached the
Grants interchange, he was confident he had the
entire sequence of mask songs fixed in his mind.

Even among a people who placed high value on
memory and who honed it in their children almost
from birth, Chee's talent was unusually strong. It had
caused his family to think of him from a very early
age as one who might become a singer. The Slow
Talking Dinee had produced more famous singers
than any of the other more than sixty Navajo clans.
And the family of his mother had produced far more
than its share. His uncle, the brother of his mother,
was among the most prominent of these. He was
Hosteen Frank Sam Nakai, who performed the Night
Chant and the Enemy Way and key parts of several
other curing ceremonials, and who sometimes taught
ceremonialism at the Navajo Community College at
Rough Rock. It was Hosteen Nakai who had chosen
Jimmy Chee's "war name," which was Long Thinker.
Thus his uncle was one of the very few who knew his
real and secret identity. His uncle had named him,
but when he had asked his uncle to teach him to be a
singer, his uncle had at first refused.

"There is a first step which must be taken," Hosteen Nakai had said. "Nothing important can happen before that." As a first step, Jimmy Chee must study the white man and the way of the white man. When he came to understand this white man's world which surrounded the People, he must make a decision. Would he follow the white man's way or would he be a Navajo?

His uncle had driven his truck into Gallup and parked it on Railroad Avenue, where they could see the bars and watch the Navajos and the Zunis going in and out of them. Jimmy Chee remembered it very well. He remembered the woman who came out of the Turquoise Tavern and the man in the black reservation hat who followed her. They had walked unsteadily, both drunk. The woman had lost her balance and sat heavily on the dirty sidewalk, and the man had bent to help her. His hat had fallen and rolled into the gutter. Hosteen Nakai's fierce eyes had watched all this.

"They cannot decide," he said. "The way Changing Woman taught us is too hard for them, and they have lost its beauty. But they do not know the white man's way. You have to decide. It is easy, now, to be a white man. You have gone to school and there are scholarships to go more, and jobs if you learn what the white man puts his value in."

Jimmy Chee had said that he had already decided. He wanted to walk in beauty as a Navajo.

"You can't decide until you understand the white man. They have much that we don't have. To be a Navajo is to have no money," Hosteen Nakai had said. "When you are older we will talk again. If you still wish it, I will begin teaching you something. But you must study the white man's way."

Chee had studied. After Shiprock High School, he had enrolled at the University of New Mexico. He'd studied anthropology, sociology, and American literature in class. Every waking moment he studied the way white men behaved. All four subjects fascinated him. When he came home during semester breaks to his mother's place in the Chuska Mountains, Hosteen Nakai taught him the wisdom of the Dinee. Finally his uncle began teaching him the ritual songs that brought the People back from their sicknesses to walk in beauty. And Chee's memory always served him well.

On the road that leads from Grants into the back side of Ambrosia Lakes uranium fields, Chee returned the recorder to its case and concentrated on finding the home of Tomas Charley. He found it some thirty feet west of the narrow asphalt pavement. It was a two-room adobe to which someone had connected a wooden frame lean-to with a roof of red composition shingles. A 1962 Chevrolet Impala squatted on cinderblock supports in the front yard, all four of its wheels missing. Chee pulled his patrol car to a stop beside it and sat waiting. If someone was home, willing to receive a visitor, he would appear at the door. If he didn't after a polite interval of waiting, Chee would knock.

The front door opened and Chee could see someone looking at him through the screen. A child. Chee waited. No one else appeared. Chee climbed out of the carryall.

"Ya-tah," he said. "Hello."

"Hello," the child said. It was a boy, about ten or twelve.

"I'm looking for Tomas Charley," Chee said.

"He went to get my mother," the boy said.

"Where's that?"

"They won't be there," the boy said. "She's a weaver. My uncle was taking her to the rug auction."

"At Crownpoint?" Chee asked.

"Yeah," the boy said. "She's going to sell a bunch of rugs."

Chee laughed. "I'm not very lucky today," he said. "That's where I came from and now I'll have to drive right back."

"You going to see my uncle there?"

"If I can find him," Chee said. "What's he driving?"

"A 1975 Ford pickup," the boy said. "An F-150. Blue. If you see him, tell him maybe somebody wants to buy our old Chevy. Tell him a man came by right after he left, looking for him," the boy said.

"Sure," Chee said. "Anything else?"

"Maybe the man will see him there at the rug auction," the boy said. "He's a blond guy, wearing a yellow jacket. He was going to look for him there."

"Okay," Chee said. He looked at the car with more interest now. The exposed brake drums were brown with rust and the upholstery in the back seat hung down in dusty festoons. Tomas Charley's nephew was overly optimistic. No one was going to drive all the way to Crownpoint to arrange to buy that junker.

12

IT WAS AFTER SUNDOWN when Chee drove past the Tribal Police office. It was dark. On the other side of the village, perhaps two hundred assorted vehicles were parked at the Crownpoint elementary school, suggesting a good turnout for the November rug auction. Chee found a blue Ford 150 pickup. Parked next to it was a green-and-white Plymouth, like the one Charley's nephew had said the would-be car buyer was driving. Chee checked it quickly. It was new, with less than three thousand miles on the odometer. A folder on the dashboard suggested it had been rented from the Albuquerque airport office of Hertz.

Inside the school, the air was rich with a mélange of aromas. Chee identified the smells of cooking fry bread, floor wax, blackboard chalk, stewing mutton and red chili, of raw wool, of horses, and of humans. In the auditorium, perhaps a hundred potential buyers were wandering among the stacks of rugs on the display tables, inspecting the offerings and noting item numbers. At this hour, most of the crowd would be in the cafeteria, eating the traditional auction dinner of Navajo tacos—tortillas topped with a lethal combination of stewed mutton and chili. Chee stood just inside the auditorium entrance, methodically examining its inhabitants. He had little idea what Charley would look like—just Becenti's sketchy description. His inspection was simply a matter of habit.

"Looking for someone?"

The voice came from beside him, from a young woman in a blue turtleneck sweater. The woman was small, the sweater large, and the face atop the folds of bulky cloth was unsmiling.

"Trying to find a man named Tomas Charley," Chee said. "But I don't know what he looks like."

The woman's face was oval, framed by soft blond hair. Her eyes were large, and blue, and intent on Chee. A pretty lady, and Chee recognized the look. He had seen it often at the University of New Mexico—and most often among Anglo coeds enrolled in Native American Studies courses. The courses attracted Anglo students, largely female, enjoying racial/ethnic guilt trips. Chee had concluded early that their interest was more in Indian males than in Indian mythology. Their eyes asked if you were really any different from the blond boys they had grown up with. Chee looked now into the eyes of the woman in the bulky blue turtleneck and detected the same question. Or thought he did. There was also something else. He smiled at her. "Not knowing what he looks like makes it tougher to find him."

"Why not just go away and leave him alone?" she asked. "What are you hunting him for?"

Chee's smile evaporated. "I have a message from his nephew," he said. "Somebody wants to buy his old car and . . ."

"Oh," the young woman said. She looked embarrassed. "I guess I shouldn't jump to conclusions. I'm sorry. I don't know him."

"I'll just ask around," Chee said. Her distaste for police was another standard reaction Chee had learned to expect from the young Anglos the reservation seemed to attract. He suspected there was a federal agency somewhere assigned to teach social workers that all police were Cossacks and that Navajo police were the worst of all. "Are you with the Bureau of Indian Affairs?" he asked.

"No," she said. "I'm helping the weavers' cooperative." She gestured vaguely toward the check-in table, where two Navajo women were sorting through papers. "But I teach school here. Fifth grade. English and social studies." The hostility was gone from her eyes now. The curiosity remained.

"I'm Jim Chee." He extended his hand. "I've been assigned to the police station here. Fairly new here."

"I noticed your uniform," she said. She took his extended hand. "Mary Landon," she said. "I'm new, too. From Wisconsin, but I taught last spring at Laguna Pueblo school."

"How do you do," Chee said. Her hand was small and cool in his, and very quickly withdrawn.

"I have to get back to work," Mary Landon said, and she was gone.

It took Chee about thirty minutes to establish that Tomas Charley was present at the auction and to get a description of the man. He might have done it faster had there been any sense of urgency. There wasn't. Chee was more involved in getting acquainted with the occupants of his territory. Then Mary Landon was at his elbow again.

"That's him," she said. "Right over there. The red-and-black mackinaw and the black felt hat."

"Thanks," Chee said. Mary Landon still wasn't smiling.

Tomas Charley was leaning against the wall alone. He seemed to be watching someone in the crowd. Mary Landon said something else, but Chee didn't hear it. He was studying Charley. He was a small man—not over five and a half feet—and skinny. His face was bony, with small, deep-set eyes and a narrow forehead under the brim of his tipped-back hat. There was an alertness about him, a tension. The eyes shifted to Chee now, quickly past him, and back again. Becenti had said he was half crazy, a fanatic. The small black eyes had the look of those who see visions. Getting Tomas Charley to talk, Chee thought, would take a lot of care and a lot of luck.

As it developed, it was no trouble at all. They talked a bit about the rug auction, and about the drought. Chee leaned against the wall beside the man, guiding the conversation. The auctioneer was on the stage now, a florid white man explaining the rules in a West Texas voice. Chee talked of Sheriff Gordo Sena, of jurisdiction problems between Navajo police and white sheriffs. The first rug was auctioned for $65. Bidding on the second one stuck at $110. The auctioneer put it aside and joked with the crowd about its stinginess. He moved the offer up to $155, and sold it.

Chee talked of Mrs. Vines' job offer, of what she'd said of the burglary, of his decision not to get involved in it, and of Vines' withdrawing the offer. Tomas Charley said less and less.

"It's no business of mine," Chee said. "I don't care about the burglar." He grinned at Charley. "I know who went in Vines' house and got that box. You know who went in. And Gordo Sena never is going to know. What I'd like to know is what was in that box."

Charley said nothing. Chee waited. On the fifth rug, bidding was spirited. The auctioneer sold it for $240.

"I've got a curious mind," Chee said. "Lots of things funny about Vines. Lots of things funny about Gordo Sena. Mrs. Vines, too."

Tomas Charley glanced at him, then glanced away. He stood with his arms crossed in front of him. The fingers of his left hand, Chee noticed, tapped nervously against his right wrist.

"Why did Vines bury your grandfather there at his house?" Chee asked. "I wonder about that. And why did somebody try to kill your father? And why did Mrs. Vines want me to find Vines' old box? And then not want me to find it? And why did Gordo Sena warn me to mind my own business?"

Chee asked the last question directly to Charley. The drumming fingers stopped. Charley pursed his lips.

"I don't give a damn if you got into Vines' house and took something," Chee said. "None of my business. But what was in that box?"

"Rocks," Tomas Charley said. "Chunks of black rocks."

It occurred to Chee that he hadn't really thought about what the box might hold. But he hadn't expected this. He considered it. "No papers?" he asked. "Nothing with anything written on it?"

"Mostly rocks," Charley said.

"Nothing else?"

"Some medals," Charley said. "Stuff from the war. Stuff like that." He shrugged.

"Tell me everything that was in it."

Charley looked surprised. "Well," he said. "There's a little card glued inside the lid. Got Vines' name and address on it. Then there was three medals. One was the Purple Heart and the other two were like stars. One out of some kind of brown metal and the other one looked about the same, but it had a little silver star in the middle of it. And there was a set of wings like paratroopers wear, and a shoulder patch with an eagle head on it and silver bars like lieutenants wear in the army." Charley thought. "Photographs. A picture of a girl, and a picture of a man and woman standing by an old car, and then a whole bunch of black rocks." Charley stopped. The catalog was complete.

"Nothing else?" Chee asked. "What did you expect to find?"

Charley shrugged.

"Luck?" Chee asked.

Charley's face tightened. "Vines was a witch," he said. He didn't use the Navajo word, which meant witch, or skinwalker, or Navajo Wolf. He used a Keresan expression—the word the people of Laguna and Acoma used to mean sorcerer.

"I heard that, too," Chee said. "You think you'd find his medicine bundle?"

Charley glanced at Chee, then looked away. Time ticked past. The auctioneer began the rhythmic litany of another transaction.

"He was killing my father," Charley said. "I wanted to turn the witching around. I wanted to find something for that."

Chee didn't say any of the obvious things. He didn't say, "Your father is dying of cancer." He didn't say, "It's not witchcraft; it's something wrong with the way the cells grow." He said nothing at all. Tomas Charley was sure his father had been doomed by a witch. When that happened, the Navajo way was a ceremonial—usually the Enemy Way or the Prostitution Way. Each invoked a traditional formula which reversed the witchcraft and turned it against the witch. And each required something that the witch had used. But Tomas Charley was half Laguna. He saw Vines as the Lagunas saw sorcerers.

Perhaps they had a different formula. The auctioneer completed his transaction, selling a small dia-
mond-patterned rug to a woman using bidding card
72. Chee and Tomas Charley leaned against the wall,
watching, their shoulders touching.

"Why was Vines witching your father?" Chee
asked. "Do you know that?"

"Vines wasn't always a sorcerer," Charley said.
"Once he was a good man, I think, and he helped my
grandfather and he helped our church. He gave us
our totem. He gave it to my grandfather. The mole.
It is powerful, and it helps the Lord Peyote open the
door for us. It helps bring us visions. Vines wanted
to get it back. So he made my father sick. And then
he stole my father's body."

On the stage, the auctioneer and his assistant
held up a saddle blanket. "This un's a dandy," the
Texan was saying. He leaned comically against its
pretended weight. "Take a stout horse to carry this
un. Wove so tight you couldn't get water through it.
I'm starting at eighty. Yum at eighty. Eighty.
Eighty. Yum at eighty. Eighty-five. Have eighty-five.
Yum at eighty-five. Ninety. Yum at ninety."

"Stole your father's body?" Chee asked. He was
thinking Emerson Charley had been alive last week.
Very sick but alive. How long ago was it? Five days?
Six? He glanced at Charley. The thin man was staring straight ahead, every line in his face rigid. He
seemed to be remembering something.

"When did Vines steal your father's body?"

"Two, three days ago," Charley said. "Out of the

hospital there at Albuquerque. And he got the mole back again."

"But how did he do it? Did he just walk in and walk out with it?"

Charley shrugged. "Vines is a witch," he said. "The hospital, they call me, and they tell me my father died and what to do with the body? When I get there, Vines had already got off with it. That's all I know."

"What was the hospital's explanation?"

"They didn't know what happened. Just the body was gone. One man told me that some of the kinfolks must have got a funeral home to get it. He said the body was put where they put the bodies, and the next day it was gone. He said it must have been a funeral home got it."

"You reported it to the police?"

"Yeah," Charley said. "They didn't do nothing."

They wouldn't, Chee thought. He imagined Charley showing up at the Albuquerque police building, trying to find somebody to take the report, telling a clerk (would the clerk have been incredulous, or merely bored?) of a missing body taken by a witch. What would the crime have been? At worst, transporting a cadaver without a permit from the medical examiner. And the police would have guessed it was merely a mix-up: the body claimed by another relative, a family feud perhaps. And Tomas Charley wouldn't have raised hell and pressed for answers. He already knew two answers. One was that nobody would pay much attention to a Navajo trying to raise hell. And the other was that a witch had flown away with the body. Still, Chee felt his anger rising at this indignity.

"Those sons-a-bitches," he said. "You want me to try to find him for you?"

Charley thought about it.

"Well," he said. "I'm half Acoma and half Navajo, and I guess I'm Navajo far as bodies go. When the old man died, he died. Body don't mean nothing but trouble. But my mother, she's Acoma. She'd like to know he's buried the right way. She wouldn't want a witch to have him."

"I'll see what I can do," Chee said. "Why do you think Vines got him?"

Charley hesitated. "It's got to do with our church," he said. "I got to go way back to explain it."

Tomas Charley went back to World War II, when his grandfather was working on the Santa Fe Railroad track crew, and had met an Indian from Oklahoma, and had been introduced to the Native American Church and Lord Peyote. His grandfather had founded a church in the Checkerboard country, and one day Lord Peyote had opened the door so his grandfather could see God. He was working then on an oil well, and God told him that something bad would happen the next day and to tell his crew not to go to work. The oil well had blown up just as God had warned and the word had spread among the Navajos and the Laguna-Acomas of this miracle, and the grandfather's congregation grew. By the next year more than two hundred people were coming to the Peyote Ways. Then one time a white man came. He was a uranium prospector named Benjamin Vines. Vines told everyone at the Peyote Way that the Lord Peyote had given him a dream of where to find uranium ore.

"All this is the way my father told me," Charley said. "He said Vines came back about a month later and told my grandfather the uranium ore was where the Lord Peyote said it would be. They had another Peyote Way and Vines had another vision. This time Lord Peyote told Vines he had now done two miracles for my grandfather's church. He had saved the men from the explosion, and he had led Vines to the ore. He said Vines was blessed, and those men he had saved were blessed, and since the blessing had come from under the ground, from an oil well and uranium ore, their totem would be the mole and their name would be the name of the moles—the People of Darkness."

"And Vines gave your grandfather a mole fetish?"

"A little later," Charley said. "They didn't have a Way for a while because the Navajo Police and the BIA cops were arresting everybody and searching people for peyote buttons, and Gordo Sena was after everybody in the church. But then they had a Way at a secret place, and Vines gave these mole fetishes to my grandfather and to the other men who Lord Peyote had saved." Charley paused. "That was before Vines got to be a witch," he explained.

"How'd that happen?" Chee asked.

"First my grandfather got sick," Charley said. "They had a sing for him, but it didn't help very long. He went into the hospital. In and out a lot. Finally he died and Vines buried him up at his ranch. He was just building that big house then. The church sort of died out then for years. Then my father got it going again. After that, Vines came around. He tried to get my father to give him the medicine bundle, the box for Lord Peyote, the mole totem, all of the sacred things. My father wouldn't give them up. After that Vines didn't come to the Peyote Way again."

That seemed to be the end of the story. Charley slumped against the wall, looking across the crowded auditorium toward the stage. The Texan had just sold a small yellow *yei* rug to number 18 for forty-five dollars and was describing a black-and-gray diamond design from Two Gray Hills as "worth three hundred dollars in any trading post on the reservation."

"Then what?" Chee prodded.

Charley didn't say anything for a moment. "Then we started hearing things."

"Like what?"

"Hearing Vines was a witch."

There was another pause. The Navajo half of Charley seemed to be ascendant, Chee thought. Navajos did not like to talk about witches.

"Tell you what," Chee said. "You don't want that old box of Vines' with the rocks in it. You let me know where to look, and we'll get it back to the owner. If anybody asks how we found it, it was an anonymous telephone call."

"It's out in the malpais," Charley said. "It was locked. I took it to a place out there where I go and pried it open. It was heavy, so I just left it there." He explained to Chee how to find it. "I got to go now," he said. "I've got to work tomorrow."

"Did the man see you about buying that old Chevy?"

Charley looked surprised. "No," he said. "Somebody want to buy that?"

"That's what your nephew said. He said to tell you a man came looking for you, and he wanted to buy that old car, and he was going to look for you here."

"Must be crazy," Charley said. And he walked away.

And I must be crazy, too, Chee thought as he watched Charley move down the aisle toward the table where an association clerk was paying off rug weavers for their sales. Rocks in a keepsake box. B. J. Vines as mystic prophet. B. J. Vines as witch. A body lost out of a hospital morgue. And Chee wasting his time in an affair that made no sense at all.

He wasted more time watching the auction, moving among the spectators idly at first and then looking for Mary Landon. She was interested in him, of that he was sure. He was equally sure that it was nothing very personal. The interest was more generic than individual. Another Navajo male, adequately scrubbed and trimmed, would have been just as interesting to the blue-eyed woman. Fair enough.

At the moment, he was particularly interested in whites, and white women. The Navajo women he knew—his mother, her two sisters, who were his "little mothers," the Navajo girls he'd been involved with—did nothing to explain Rosemary Vines. And he'd never really known the white girls. Their curiosity had put him off. But Mary Landon he would study. Unfortunately, Mary Landon was nowhere to be seen.

He walked into the parking lot, savoring the cold fresh air after the stuffy heat inside. Tomas Charley was standing beside his truck, talking to a white man in a yellow windbreaker. The white man was blond. The buyer of worthless rusty Chevrolets had found his man. Chee stared at him, curious. The white man seemed to feel the eyes on him. He stared back. The same man, Chee realized, had been watching him and Charley in their long conversation against the wall. Mary Landon was still invisible.

He found her, finally, in the cafeteria kitchen helping a half-dozen other women with cleanup operations.

"The message is delivered," Chee said. "Thanks."

It was the third time he had spoken to her, and Chee had a theory about third meetings between people. The third time you were no longer strangers.

"It must have been a long message," Mary said. "I think you found something to talk about besides someone wanting to buy a car." The words were skeptical, but after she said them she smiled.

Chee found himself trying to think of something

to ask her, of a reason to be in this kitchen talking to her. His mind was blank. "How about having a cup of coffee?" he heard himself saying. "The coffee shop will be open late."

The first time she had looked at him she had been inspecting a Tribal Police sergeant. Now she was looking at a man asking her out for coffee. It was a different sort of inspection. "I have to finish with these pots," she said.

"I'll do it for you," Chee said.

Chee washed dishes each evening in his mobile home—a plate, cup, knife, and fork left over from breakfast, a second plate, a cup, and cutlery from dinner, and the frying pan used to cook both meals. But never since his university days had he washed dishes socially.

"You look like you enjoy that," Mary said. "Maybe you missed your calling."

Chee tried to think of something witty. He couldn't.

In the booth at the Crownpoint Café, Chee learned a little about Mary Landon, and she learned a little about him. She had come to Laguna the previous year to replace a teacher hurt in an automobile accident. Then she had landed the Crownpoint job. She was from a little place not far from Milwaukee. She had attended the University of Wisconsin. She liked canoeing and hiking, and the outdoors in general. She didn't like pretentious people. She liked teaching Navajo children, but wasn't sure what to do about their conditioning against competitiveness.

She hoped to learn Navajo, but it was hard to pro-
nounce and so far she could speak only a few
phrases. She spoke them, and Chee pretended to understand, and Mary Landon was not fooled by the
pretense but appreciated it and rewarded him with
a genuinely friendly look. Chee asked her about her
parents, and learned her father ran a sporting goods
store. He decided not to ask her about her hostility
to police. This wasn't the time for that, and the attitude was common enough.

Mary Landon learned Chee was one of the Slow
Talking Dinee, the clan of his mother, and was "born
to" the Bitter Water Dinee, the clan of his father.
She learned that Chee's father was dead, that his
maternal uncle was a noted *yataalii,* and she had
been around Navajo country long enough to know
about the role of these shamans in the ceremonial
life of the People. She learned a good deal more
about his family, ranging from his two older sisters
through a galaxy of cousins, uncles, and aunts, one
of whom represented the Greasy Water district on
the Tribal Council.

"She's my mother's sister, which makes her my
'little mother,'" Chee said. "A real tiger."

"You're not playing the game," Mary Landon
said. "I told you about me. You're just telling me
about your family."

The statement surprised Chee. One defined himself by his family. How else? And then it occurred to
him that white people didn't. They identified themselves by what they had done as individuals. He

added sugar to his coffee, thinking about it.

"That's the way we play the game. If I was introducing you to Navajos, I wouldn't say, 'This is Mary Landon, who teaches at Crownpoint,' and so forth. I'd say, 'This woman is a member of . . .'—your mother's family, and your father's family—and I'd tell about your uncles and aunts, so everyone would know just exactly where you fit in with the people around you."

"'This woman'?" Mary Landon asked. "You wouldn't tell them my name?"

"That would be rude. Now more people have English names, but among traditional Navajos it's very impolite to say someone's name in their presence. Names are just reference words, when the person's not there."

Mary Landon looked incredulous. "I think that's . . ." She stopped.

"Silly?" Chee asked. "You have to understand the system. Our real names are secret. We call them war names. Somebody very close to you in the family names you when you're little. Something that fits your personality, if possible. Not more than a half-dozen people are ever going to know it. It's used for ceremonial purposes: if a girl is having her *kinaalda*—her puberty ceremony—or if you're having a sing done for you. Then, as you grow, people give you nicknames to refer to you. Like 'Cry Baby,' and 'Hard Runner,' or maybe 'Long Hands' or 'Ugly.'" Chee laughed. "I've got an uncle on my father's side everybody calls 'Liar.'"

"How about Jim Chee? Isn't that your real name?"

"Along came the trading posts," Chee said. "Along came the white man. He had to have a name to write down when one of us pawned our jewelry to him, or got credit for groceries. The traders started formalizing the nicknames, and before long we had to have names on birth certificates, so you got family names, like mine. I've had nicknames, too. Two or three. And I'm sure you do, too."

"Me?" Mary Landon looked surprised.

"How long you been at Crownpoint? Three months? Sure. The people have a name for you by now."

"Like what?"

"Something that fits. Maybe 'Pretty Teacher.' Or 'Stubborn Girl.'" Chee shrugged. "'Blue Eyes.' 'Blond Woman.' 'Fast Talker.' Do you want me to find out for you?"

"Sure," she said. Then, "No, wait. Maybe just forget it. How about you? What do they call you?"

"Here? I don't know. When I was at Rough Rock they used to call me . . ." He paused, and then said the word carefully in Navajo. "It means 'One Who Studies to Be a Singer.'"

"Oh," Mary Landon said. "Are you?"

"I was," Chee said. "I guess I still am, in a way. It depends."

"On what?"

"I applied for admission to the FBI. More or less to see how I'd do. Took the tests. Got interviewed by the screening panel at Albuquerque. Last week I got a letter telling me I'd been accepted. I'm supposed to report to the academy in Virginia. December tenth."

She looked at him curiously. "So you're going to be an FBI agent."

"I don't know," Chee said.

"You haven't decided?"

"What's the rush? We work on Navajo time." Even as he said it, the flippancy sounded false. December 10 wasn't Navajo time. It was four weeks away. A specific, ironclad, unbendable deadline.

"But you can't be both a Navajo medicine man and an FBI agent?"

"Not really," Chee said. He wanted to change the subject, wanted not to talk about it. As a matter of fact, you couldn't be both a Navajo and an FBI agent. You couldn't be a Navajo away from the People. "By the way," he said, "thanks for helping with Tomas Charley. I learned what I needed to know. If he told me the truth, that is."

Mary Landon studied him. Chee remembered, belatedly, what he had told her about why he wanted to find Charley.

"Do people lie a lot in your business?"

The question sounded innocent. And if it was, the answer was yes, a lot of people lie to a policeman. But Chee sensed the barb. And the answer was different.

"I'm sorry about that," he said. "I did tell his nephew I'd pass on the message about the car. But I also wanted to see him about police business."

"And you couldn't tell me that." It was more a statement than a question, and the proper answer, of course, was "No, I couldn't." But Chee sensed the hostility again (or perhaps it could now better be described as a mixture of caution and suspicion), and he was not in the mood to give the proper answer.

"I could tell you, but only if you don't mind complicated accounts of things that don't amount to much," Chee said. "Do you want to hear about it?"

She did. Chee told her about Vines, and Mrs. Vines, and the stolen keepsake box, and Sheriff Gordo Sena, and about the People of Darkness and the disappearing body, and finally about where Tomas Charley had left the box.

"And when you look at it all with a detached view," Chee said, "you see a Navajo cop simply exercising his curiosity. A crime of no particular importance. A total lack of jurisdiction."

"But it is curious," she said. "What do you think happened to Mr. Charley's father? And what are you going to do next?"

"I don't know about the body. Probably lost by the bureaucracy somehow and nobody cared enough to find it. As for me, next I'll go out in the malpais when I have some time and get the box and take a look at those rocks, and then I'll get the box back to Vines. He says he doesn't want his box back. But he must want those medals."

"What will you tell Vines?"

"I won't. I'll call the sheriff's office at Grants and tell them I got an anonymous tip on where the box had been left, and went out and found it, and for them to tell the Vineses to come and get it if they want it back."

Mary Landon raised her eyebrows and sipped her coffee.

"Okay," Chee said. "It's a lie. But how else does Vines get his box back without Charley getting in jail?"

"I can't think of a way," she said. "Something else puzzles me. How did Charley know he could trust you?"

Chee shrugged. "Because I look trustworthy?" he asked.

She laughed. "As a matter of fact, you don't," she said. "Could I go along when you go hunting the box?"

"Sure," Chee said. "We'll go tomorrow."

The apartments the Crownpoint school district provided for its teachers were a quarter mile beyond the school. The school was dark now, and the parking lot empty except for a single pickup truck. The pickup was a blue Ford 150. Charley's. Chee slowed his carryall, staring at it.

"Not here," Mary Landon said. "It's those apartments up ahead."

"I know," Chee said. "I'll get you home in just a minute."

He pulled into the parking lot, beside the pickup. "This is Charley's truck," he said. "Why would he leave it?"

The truck was locked. Frost was turning the windshield opaque. Chee walked around it, shone his flashlight into the cab, looking for anything that would answer that question. He didn't find it.

13

MALPAIS, TRANSLATED LITERALLY from the Spanish, means "bad country." In New Mexico, it signifies specifically those great expanses of lava flow which make black patches on the map of the state. The malpais of the Checkerboard country lies just below Mount Taylor, having been produced by the same volcanic fault that, a millennium earlier, had thrust the mountain fifteen thousand feet into the sky. Now the mountain has worn down to a less spectacular eleven thousand feet and relatively modern eruptions from cracks at its base have sent successive floods of melted basalt flowing southward for forty miles to fill the long valley between Cebolleta Mesa and the Zuni Mountains. Some of this malpais was ancient, long since softened by algae, moss, rain, wind, and durable desert grasses. Elsewhere it was only a few thousand years old, still raw, black, and relatively lifeless. The track Chee was following zigzagged its way across a smoother, more ancient flow. Nonetheless, it was rough going.

"I've never been out here before," Mary Landon said. "Not out in it. It's like someone was boiling a whole oceanful of black ink, and all of a sudden it froze solid."

"Even the rodents out here tend to be black," Chee said. "Protective coloration, I guess."

"It doesn't look like there'd be anything alive."

"Lots of reptiles," Chee said. "All kinds of snakes and lizards. And quite a few mammals. Rabbits, mice, kangaroo rats, so forth."

"What do they drink?" Mary asked.

"Some of them don't. They get their water from the plants they eat. But rain and snow melt and collect in potholes," Chee said. "And now and then there's a spring. That's where we're going. Charley has a spring out here. He collects herbs, datura, stuff like that. For his ceremonials. That's where he left the box."

"How do you find it?"

"Either by the powers of deduction," Chee said. "or by asking Charley. I asked Charley and he told me to follow this track until I came to the place where the new lava flow crosses the old." Chee pointed ahead. "Like right there. And then I'd see a place where the track forks. See? Right there ahead. And the spring was maybe a hundred yards down the right fork of the track. He said there was a bunch of tamarisk sticking up out of the lava flow to mark it. See? Over there."

"So why aren't you taking the right turn?" Mary asked.

"I want to show you that new lava up close," Chee said. "We'll park there and we can walk over."

The new lava was at least a thousand years old. It looked as if it had hardened yesterday. It was as black as coal, raw and rough, still marked with the froth of its white-hot bubbling as it boiled across the landscape. They climbed from the ancient lava onto the final wave of the new and stood looking across ten miles of tumbled, ragged blackness at the blue shape of Cebolleta Mesa.

"I'm impressed," Mary said finally. "It's like looking backward a hundred million years."

"Do you know any of our legends?" Chee asked.

"I know a few," Mary said. "A Laguna girl I know told me one about the Laguna migrations. And the Corn Maidens."

"Those are Pueblo," Chee said. "If you were Navajo you'd know that you are looking at the blood of the Horned Monster."

"Oh. Black blood." Mary grinned at Chee. "You Navajos have black-hearted monsters."

"Yes, indeed. A historic spot. Right around here is where the Hero Twins started making Dinetah safe for the Dinee to live in. The Horned Monster was the first one they bagged. Born of Water distracted him, and Monster Slayer shot him with an arrow."

"He certainly bled a lot," Mary said.

"And then they cleaned the rest of them out," Chee said. He helped her down from the lava crest. "The Winged Monster, and the Water Monster. We even had one they called One Who Kicks People Over the Cliff."

"How'd they do him in?"

"His hair grew out of the cliff, keeping him from falling," Chee said. "Monster Slayer gave him a haircut."

The ancient lava flow made fairly easy walking. Eons of time had rubbed away its roughness and turned its blackness gray. It was coated with lichens, and grass grew wherever dust had accumulated in its cracks. Chee talked of Navajo mythology. Mary Landon listened. He was carrying a grocery sack which contained a thermos of coffee, two apples, and two king-sized Lottaburgers picked up in Grants. Chee hadn't been on a picnic since school days. He was happy. To their right, the morning sun reflected off the snow on the high slopes of Mount Taylor, making it glitter against the dark-blue sky.

"We call it Turquoise Mountain," Chee said. "First Man built it out of earth he brought up from the Third World, and he pinned it to the world with a magic knife to keep it from flying away. He put Turquoise Girl on top of it, to keep the Navajos safe from monsters, and he assigned Big Snake to live on the mountain for eternity, to keep Turquoise Girl safe from whatever bothers Turquoise Girls."

"Speaking of big snakes," Mary Landon said. "Am I right in remembering that they hibernate in the winter, and I therefore have absolutely nothing to worry about? Or is that hibernation business just another of your myths?"

She was climbing a great hump of lava. Just beyond it were the tamarisks and the spring. "When are you going to tell me your war name?"

"It's a good rule to stay off those humps when you're walking on lava," Chee said. "They're the tops of old bubbles, and about one in twenty thousand is thin enough so that you can fall through and . . ."

Chee's voice trailed away. Mary had stopped atop the hump and stood frozen, looking down.

"Jim," she said. "There's someone . . ."

Chee scrambled up beside her.

Just beyond the hump was a sinkhole, a circle of clear, dark water rimmed by cattails and a species of green reed. This was surrounded, in turn, by a small expanse of buffalo grass. The man wore a red-and-black mackinaw and his black hat lay beside his head. His hands were together behind his back, secured by what seemed to be an electric cord.

"I think he's dead," Mary Landon said in a very small voice.

"I'll see," Chee said. The left hand looked distorted, and coated with something dark. "I think you should wait in the truck."

"All right," Mary said.

The kneeling man was Tomas Charley. The black on his hand was blood, long dried. But when Chee placed his fingers on Charley's neck to confirm the certainty that he was dead, he found the flesh resilient and warm. He stepped quickly back from the body and studied the area around him. Tomas Charley had been dead only a matter of minutes. Chee became intensely aware that his pistol, inappropriate for a picnic with a girl, was locked in the glove box of the patrol car. Perhaps Tomas Charley had been left here hours ago and had been a long time dying. And perhaps he had been killed only moments ago, which would mean his killer must be nearby. Chee glanced at the body again. There was no sign of what had killed him. The only blood visible was from the hand. Chee grimaced. The hand had been methodically mutilated. He examined the mackinaw, looking in vain for a bullet hole. Then he noticed a place where the black hair on the back of Charley's head had been scorched. He knelt beside the body and gently parted the hair. Beneath it, the skin over the skull had been punctured, leaving a small round hole. A bullet hole, probably no larger than a .22. Turquoise Girl had not kept this half-Navajo safe from the monsters.

The sound of the car starting was close. It came from beyond the tamarisks. Chee trotted around the pool toward it, conscious that the driver was probably armed. The car, he saw when he reached the screen of brush, was a green-and-white Plymouth—the one that had been parked beside Charley's car. It was moving away from him down the track. He couldn't see the driver. Chee turned and scrambled up the lava formation. When the Plymouth reached the place where the tracks forked, it would angle left, back toward the highway and Grants. Then Chee could see the driver. And he would need only a glimpse to confirm what he already knew. It would be the blond man in the yellow jacket.

But the Plymouth didn't angle left. It turned right and jolted slowly toward Chee's patrol car.

He could see Mary at the passenger-side window, looking at the approaching car and then at him.

He cupped his hands and shouted: "Run. Mary. Run."

She emerged from the driver's-side door, running toward the new lava flow. She was carrying his 30-30 carbine. Chee raced toward the patrol car, doing what he could to keep out of sight behind the humps and hillocks of old lava. The Plymouth stopped and the driver got out. He was a blond man wearing a yellow jacket, and he raised his right arm and aimed the pistol he held at Mary Landon. It seemed to Chee to have a remarkably long and heavy barrel. The barrel smoked, or seemed to, but Chee heard nothing. Mary was in the new lava and out of sight. Chee's plan took no thought at all. He would circle around the patrol car, find Mary in the new lava, and get the rifle. The blond man would think he was armed and wouldn't come after him. The risks were relatively light. In the first place, the chances of being hit at one hundred yards by a pistol were small, unless the man was a hell of a lot better shot than most. And in the second place, a .22 bullet at that range wouldn't be lethal. Chee ran.

The pain was sudden and intense. Chee stumbled, lost his footing, and fell to his hands and knees. The pain was in his left chest. A heart attack, he thought for one illogical moment. And then he felt blood running down his side and made a quick inspection. A bullet seemed to have struck a rib. He inspected the place with cautious fingers and grimaced with the pain. The bullet had apparently broken the bone. But he didn't seem to be hurt in any critical way. No reason to change his plans, except for a more realistic view of the blond man's marksmanship. He raised himself cautiously. He'd locate his adversary exactly, and then he'd resume his run toward the new lava, on a wider, safer circle.

The blond man was trotting directly toward him across the worn waves of gray stone, the long-barreled pistol held in front of him. Chee ducked. The blond either didn't care if the Navajo policeman was armed, or knew that he wasn't. Perhaps he had seen that Chee wasn't wearing his holster. And now he came to finish the job, as he had finished it with Tomas Charley. Chee felt panic, choked it off, and started a scrambling zigzag run. He'd worry about reaching Mary Landon and his rifle later. Now the problem was to stay alive, to put some distance between himself and the blond, to find a place to hide. He vaulted over a ridge of stone and heard the sharp snap of a bullet whipping past him. He heard no gunshot. Behind the ridge, the lava had hardened into a wide trough perhaps five feet deep. Chee sprinted down it, the rib feeling like a knife in his chest. Then he heard the booming crack of a shot, and the whine of a ricocheting bullet. And then another, and another. Those were not the blond's silent .22. It was the muzzle blast of his 30-30. The trough ended at a grassy pothole catch basin. He was back at Emerson Charley's spring. Chee stopped and looked over the rim. The blond man was moving back toward his car, keeping low in a dodging run. From the escarpment of new lava, Chee saw a puff of blue smoke and heard again the cracking boom of the 30-30. Then the blond was behind Chee's patrol car. For a moment Chee lost sight of him. Then he was visible again, getting into the Plymouth. The Plymouth backed around the patrol car with a squeal of tires on rock and then was jolting down the track, far faster than was safe for tires or springs.

About then Chee realized that his patrol car was burning. The flames came from under the rear of it, apparently fed by fuel leaking out of the gas tank. The fire mushroomed abruptly, engulfing the rear half of the vehicle. Chee watched it grimly. The tank was about half full as he remembered it—perhaps twelve gallons. There was another twenty in the auxiliary tank. When that heated up, it would go off like a bomb.

What had been Tomas Charley still knelt, forehead to grass. Chee walked past the body and picked up the sack containing the thermos of coffee and the picnic lunch. They had a long walk ahead of them. He spent another few minutes making a methodical search of the spring area for the box. Charley had said he'd left it in plain view on the rock just beside the water. There was no box now. Behind him, he heard the muffled boom of the gas tank exploding.

"Boy," Mary Landon said when he walked up.

"You Navajos give exciting picnics." She laughed, but it was a shaky laugh. The fire flared up again with a *whoosh* of flame as a front tire exploded, and she raised her hand to shade her face from the heat. Her sleeve was torn and her wrist was smeared with blood from a long scratch on her forearm.

"You all right?" he asked. "Thank God you took the rifle with you."

"I knew you'd say that." Suddenly Mary Landon was furious. "Why wouldn't I take it? Because I was stupid, that would be why. I'd just seen a tied-up dead body, and the man who must have killed him coming right toward me, and you yelling at me to run, and the rifle right there in the scabbard. Why wouldn't I take it?" Her voice was fierce. "Because I'm a half-wit woman? I wouldn't have said that if you'd taken the rifle. I'd take it for granted. But no. I'm a woman, so I'm stupid."

"Sorry," Chee said.

"What's wrong with this damned rifle anyway?" Mary said. She handed it to him, which reminded Chee that his spare ammunition was in the glove box and would be exploding any minute.

"Let's back away a little," he said. As he said it, the 30-30 rounds began exploding, no louder than firecrackers.

"I'm a pretty good shot, I thought," Mary said. "I was missing him a mile."

"Sorry about that, too," Chee said. "When I'm not using it I let the rear sight down." He showed her, pushing the leaf sight up with his thumb and sliding the calibrated wedge forward to the 200-yard mark.

Mary looked from Chee's thumb to Chee's face, her glance asking: Is this man for real? She shook her head. "Why? Why would you do that?"

"Takes the strain off the spring," Chee said lamely.

Suddenly she leaned against him. He felt her shaking. "Sorry I've been so bitchy," she said, talking into his coat. "I'm not used to this."

"Me either," Chee said.

"That man back there. Was that Mr. Charley? The one you were looking for? He was dead, wasn't he? Did that blond man kill him? Do you know what's going on?"

"Yes," Chee said. "And no. It was Charley. He was dead. And I don't have any idea what the hell is going on."

While he was saying it, Mary became aware of the blood on his shirt. Childish as he knew it was, being wounded made him feel a little less foolish. If the rib hadn't hurt so much, and if he hadn't had a five-mile walk back to the highway ahead of him, it would have been almost worthwhile.

14

COLTON WOLF had left tracks. Two witnesses had seen him. Close and clearly. They could
identify him. They could connect him with murder
and with a rented car. The car-rental connection
would provide other witnesses and uncover the false
identity. He gunned the Plymouth down the access
acceleration lane and onto Interstate 40 west. There
was no time wasted deciding what to do. He'd decided that before he'd left his trailer. This was Plan
B. Plan B was what he did if the operation created
the sort of disturbance that made the routine with-
drawal in some way risky. There had been a Plan B
and variations of Plan B for each of his previous
operations. But he'd never used one before because
there had never been a disturbance. Previously, the
targets had died unobserved, quietly and unobtru-
sively. The only exception had been the old CPA in
Reno. The man had suspected something. Perhaps it
had been the product of a guilty conscience, perhaps
the product of age and wisdom. At any rate, part of

the information provided to Colton had been the detail that the target would be alert and wary. And he had been. Colton had spent an extra day scouting because of that. And the set-up had seemed perfect. The accountant's office had been on the fifth floor of a downtown bank building. At midmorning for three consecutive days the old man had emerged from his office, crossed the corridor to the men's rest room, and relieved himself. Rest rooms were ideal. And this had been the best kind. A single-stall men's room. The jimmy blade flicking the latch open. The victim startled, embarrassed, refusing to credit what his eyes were telling him—that the intruder upon his privacy was pointing a pistol at his forehead. The victim starting to blurt some banality like "This booth is occupied." The voice being stopped by the *thud* of the silenced .22. The bullet fired into the hair, where it would go undetected for a time. The body propped on the stool. The unhurried departure. But this time it had been different. The old man had sensed something when Colton had come into the room. Through the gap beside the booth door, Colton had seen a single eye peering out at him, and the screaming had started the moment the jimmy touched the latch. The man was up from the stool, pants around ankles, trying to resist. It had taken three bullets and a little more time, and then, as he was propping up the body, the door had swung open and the old man's secretary had burst in. He had shot her twice, and wedged her body in with the old man's, and walked away. It had been tense for a moment, but when he emerged from the elevator, there had been absolutely no tracks left behind. He had dumped the pistol by opening the emergency hatch and putting it on top of the elevator car. When he stepped through the doors into the bank lobby, there was no chance of connecting him with the bodies in the men's room. He had hated to lose the pistol, but it couldn't be traced. There had been absolutely no tracks.

This time there were tracks everywhere. He drove west on Interstate 40 past the Grants interchange, thinking about them. Out here tracks were easy to follow. Too few people in too much space. Had all gone smoothly, Colton would have driven back to Albuquerque, checked in the car at the airport, picked up his truck, and returned to his trailer. That was Plan A, simple and quick. Then, after a few days, he would have hitched the trailer to the truck and moved along. Somewhere warmer. Maybe Houston, or maybe somewhere in California. It didn't matter where. Until he could find his mother. Then there would be a home place. A place to settle.

But now he had to use Plan B. That took him in the other direction—to Gallup. There he would check the car into a garage for a major tune-up, leaving a Gallup number to be called when repairs were completed and telling the mechanic that there wasn't any hurry. That would mean days before the car surfaced. He'd walk to the bus station, take the next bus to Phoenix, and fly back to Albuquerque.

He drove exactly five miles above the speed

limit—the margin highway patrolmen allow. There was no serious hurry. He'd bought himself some hours by burning the policeman's car and radio. He'd wounded the man, probably in the abdomen. And it would take the woman at least three hours to walk out of the lava rock and turn in the alarm. By the time any serious search could be organized, he'd be well into Arizona. Outside the circle.

A semi-trailer rig breezed past him, going perhaps fifteen miles above the limit. That would mean the trucker's CB had assured him he was safe from the state police. But Colton held the rental Plymouth at a steady sixty. He was thinking how he would erase his tracks. Not since he was a boy had Colton felt so vulnerable. He knew the Indian policeman had seen him at the auction, clearly and close up. The policeman and the woman had seen him again on the lava. The policeman and the woman had to be killed just as quickly as Colton could manage it.

15

THE WAY JIMMY CHEE was propped against the pillows, he could shift his eyes to the left and look out the window of his fifth-floor room in the Bernalillo County Medical Center and see, across Lomas Avenue, the tan book tower of the University of New Mexico library and the modern-sculpture form of the Humanities Building. If he shifted his eyes to the right, he'd see on the TV screen the has-beens and never-would-bes of *Hollywood Squares* pretending to enjoy themselves. The TV screen was silent, the sound turned off. All Chee could hear was the voice of Sheriff Gordo Sena, whose face Chee could see when he turned his eyes straight ahead. Voice and face were angry. "What I want you to do," Sena was saying, "is drop all the bullshit. Just tell me some by-God truth for once. I want to know how you knew Tom Charley had that box. And what was in it. And what happened to it. And how come that feller in the Plymouth was after him."

And what I'd like to know, Chee was thinking, is

how Gordo Sena got past the nurse. The FBI people had come earlier, while he was trying to eat his breakfast, and the nurse had peered in at him and said, "You're not ready to talk to police, are you," and that had been the end of the FBI. But thirty minutes later, Sena had simply pushed the door open, stalked in, turned off the TV volume, sat in the bedside chair, and said, "By God, we're going to get some things straightened out." It was now about thirty questions later.

"I didn't know Charley had the box," Chee said for the third time. "It was an educated guess. I told you what Mrs. Vines told me. About thinking the burglary had a religious connection. Well, the religion is peyote, and Charley is the peyote chief. One plus one is two."

"Was," Sena corrected. *"Was* the peyote chief. So you just walk up to Charley and ask him if he's the burglar, and he admits it. That's what you're trying to get me to believe."

"That's what happened," Chee said. "Not quite, but just about." His ears were ringing, and his rib hurt, and the nausea that had come and gone all morning was coming again. He didn't feel like talking. He closed his eyes. Sena's glowering face went away, but not the voice. Question after question about why Charley had stolen the box, what Charley had said was in the box, what Charley had said about the Vineses. Questions that explored from every possible angle what Chee knew about the blond man in the green-and-white Plymouth.

"What kind of voice did he have?" Sena asked.

Chee opened his eyes. "Never talked to him." He'd told Sena that before. Twice, in fact.

"That's right, you didn't," Sena said. His alert eyes were studying Chee's face. Why did Sena think they had talked? Why was that so important to the sheriff?

More questions. Why had the blond man burned Chee's car? The answer seemed obvious to Chee, but he answered it. To prevent pursuit and the quick radio call that would have inevitably snared the Plymouth at a roadblock. Why did the blond man seem inclined to pursue Mary Landon? Obvious again. She and Chee had had a good look at the killer. He was trying to eliminate witnesses.

Sena hitched his chair closer to the bed. He leaned forward. "Did you find the box?"

"No," Chee said.

"Had Tomas Charley opened it? Did he tell you that?"

"He opened it," Chee said. They had already covered this.

"What was in it?"

Chee was dizzy. He wanted Sena to go away. The sheriff's avid face went slightly out of focus.

"Did he tell you that? What was in the box?"

"What I said; mostly just some rocks," Chee said. "A bunch of black rocks, and some old military stuff—medals, a paratroop badge, a shoulder patch, and a few old photographs of people. Family, Charley thought they were."

"Rocks?" Sena said.

"Mostly full of black rocks," Chee said.

Sena was silent. His hard dark eyes stared at Chee. "You got any brothers?"

"No," Chee said. "Two sisters. No brothers." The question surprised him.

"I had one," Sena said. "Older brother. His name was Robert. He was smart. Smartest kid in Grants High School. Made the valedictorian speech. First time in years it hadn't been some Anglo girl. Got a scholarship to the university here, but he didn't go at first. Our old man had heart trouble. Robert worked in the onion fields, in the oil fields, things like that. He looked after us kids. Took care of us. Kept us out of trouble. The old man died and left some social security, so Robert finally went to the university. He was studying engineering."

Sena had delivered that information in a flat staccato. Now his voice trailed off. He looked down at his hands, drew in a long breath, held it and then let it go. When he looked up again, his eyes were no longer hard. "I'm going to ask you a favor," he told Chee. "I don't do that much."

Chee nodded.

"I want to tell you how Robert died," Sena said. He described the oil well explosion and how the chief of the Navajo roustabout crew had kept his men away that day. "For a while I thought he did it. Now I just think he was in on it somehow. Knew about the plan. Knew Robert was going to be killed. That fella was Dillon Charley, Tomas' granddaddy."

Sena looked down at his hands. The muscles in his jaw were working.

"What do you want me to do?" Chee asked.

Sena didn't look up. "I want to know who killed Robert," he said. "I want to nail the sons of bitches. You talked to Mrs. Vines. You talked to Dillon Charley's grandson. There's some secret here that's got to do with being Indian, and with that peyote religion. One of them told you something. You've figured something out. You know more than you're telling. Otherwise, you wouldn't have found Vines' box so quick."

"I don't know a damned thing," Chee said. "Not about that oil well explosion. You think the Vineses had something to do with it?"

Sena shook his head. "He didn't live here then. And she didn't get here until his first wife died. I think Dillon Charley told Vines something. Anyway, it's a damned cinch Mrs. Vines knows something. Why else would she connect stealing that box with that bunch of peyote freaks?"

"I don't know," Chee said.

The room fell silent. An ambulance turned off Lomas toward the BCMC emergency room entrance, its siren abruptly growling out.

"Nothing to tell me, then?" Sena asked.

"Not that I haven't already told you," Chee said.

Sena pursed his lips, glanced at his watch. "It's a hell of a way to kill a man," he said. "Blowing 'em to pieces like that. We didn't hardly find enough of Robert to bury. And part of what we buried might not have been him. Had one of his legs with the boot still on it. Part of the torso we could recognize because his belt buckle was in it. Never found a lot of him. The coyotes and the buzzards and things had had a couple of days to carry it away." Sena's eyes were hard and bright, staring into Chee's eyes. His jaw muscles were rigid. "My mother used to go out there and look. She'd walk around in the creosote bush looking for pieces of bone." Sena produced a series of sounds that might have been a laugh. "I think she wanted to put Robert all back together again. What do you think of that?"

Chee could think of nothing to say. White people's attitude toward their dead was beyond his understanding.

"Two things," Sena said. "One I'm asking you, and one I'm telling. If you can tell me anything about that peyote bunch, or the Vineses, or anything that will help me, well, I'd appreciate that. I'd remember it. I never forget a favor. And two, I'm telling you to stay out of my jurisdiction. This whole business is mine. The burglary and the killing and everything else. It's mine. It's been mine for most of my life, and I don't want you in it. I told you that once, and you didn't pay attention to me." Sena's voice was shaking. He stopped talking for a moment, gaining control. "Now, I got a name for being hard," he continued. "I've killed a man or two in the line of duty, and there's some that says I've killed some that didn't need to be killed. However that is, I'll tell you this. You think you're unlucky that blond man run into you out there on the malpais. Fact is, you're lucky it wasn't me."

Sena got up and placed his chair neatly against the wall under the television set. He went through the door without a glance or a word.

On the television screen, a barrage of commercials replaced *Hollywood Squares* and gave way in turn to what seemed to be a soap opera. The screen was filled with the tear-wet face of a woman. Her lips moved soundlessly, and she dabbed at her eyes. Chee shifted his own eyes to the left, and stared out across the central campus of the University of New Mexico. He thought first about Gordo Sena's hatred. And then about the pattern of his questions. It had not been a debriefing—one officer collecting information from another. It had been an interrogation—the probing of a hostile witness, skillfully done. But exactly what had Sena wanted to learn?

Part of that was obvious. Part of it wasn't. Chee sorted it out in his mind. Three times, in three different ways, Sena had tried to learn if there had been any communication between him and the blond man. Why was that so important to Sena? Was the blond man working for the sheriff? Had Sena hired the man to get the box away from Tomas Charley? There was no way to answer that question. It would seem more logical that he had been hired by Vines.

The telephone rang. Chee groaned.

"I'm Sergeant Hunt," the voice said, "with the Albuquerque Police Department. You feel like having a visitor?"

It was a soft voice, very polite.

"Why not?" Chee said.

"You're going to have to tell that nurse, then," the voice said. "She wouldn't let me in."

"I'll tell her," Chee said.

"Be right up, then," Hunt said, and hung up.

Chee pushed the button to summon someone from the nursing station. Why would the APD send a man to talk to him? It was an FBI case, or, as Sena insisted, the Valencia County sheriff's. That would depend on whether you counted the abduction, which had happened in federal jurisdiction on the reservation, or the murder, which was probably in Sena's territory, depending on where the lines fell on the checkerboard. Either way, it would be of zero interest to the Albuquerque law.

Hunt was a small man, with pale-gray eyes and a narrow, bony face.

"Looks like you forgot to dodge," Hunt said. "In case you wondered, the bullet broke up, but it looks like a .22. Probably a hollow point."

"It looked like it might have been a .22 pistol with a silencer on the barrel," Chee said. "Felt like a cannonball."

"I've got the report you gave to the state police here," Hunt said. "Sounds like you got a pretty good look at him."

"Yeah," Chee said. "Close enough." He tried to remember what he had told the state policeman. It was all hazy. They had started to walk back to the highway. Mary Landon and he. It had quickly become slow and painful. Each step produced a stab-bing pain in his chest. Soon he had been dizzy. He had sat beside the track. Mary had spread her coat on the ground and made him lie down, and she had gone, running, intending to flag down some driver and get help. He had dozed and awakened and dozed again. Finally, when the sun was almost directly overhead, he had awakened to see a man in the black uniform of the New Mexico State Police bending over him. He remembered talking to the policeman, and Mary's worried face, and driving to the inter-state, and being transferred to an ambulance. He remembered Mary riding with him. But that was about all he remembered. Where was Mary now?

"We'd like to get another description," Hunt said. "Have you go over it again."

"Medium-sized," Chee said. "About thirty. Proba-bly weighed about 150. Five ten, probably less. Looked to be in good shape. Hair was very blond, medium short. Sort of prominent bone structure, as I remember. Strong chin, blue eyes, light eyebrows. No mustache. No beard. Light complexion. Pale. Ears fairly large and laid close to his skull."

Hunt had been making notes. Chee closed his eyes, seeing the face again as he had seen it at the auction, the light-blue eyes watching him. "I can't think of any more details. He looked smart, if you know what I mean by that."

Hunt had opened a manila folder. "He look any-thing like this?" he asked. He handed Chee a sketch done in pencil on thin white cardboard. It looked like a sketch made by a police artist. It also looked a lot like the blond man.

Chee handed it back. "Could be him," he said. "Probably is. Who is he?"

"We don't know for sure," Hunt said.

Chee's rib throbbed. He felt a sudden wave of sickness. His ears were ringing. He was not in the mood for coyness. "God damn it," he said. "Let's not play games. Who was the sketch supposed to look like? And how come it's APD business? It's a hundred miles out of your territory."

"That takes a minute to explain," Hunt said. "We have a file on old unsolved homicides in the detective division, and I'm the one who keeps track of it. You know, review it every six months or so to see if anything new fits in. Anyway, last summer we had a funny double killing. Two guys on a wrecker were going to tow an old pickup out of a reserved parking zone, and the thing blew up and killed 'em both. We got lucky and found a witness who'd been sitting at a window watching the world go by. She had seen somebody who looked like this"—Hunt tapped the sketch—"put a package in the back of the pickup before it went boom."

"Ah," Chee said. He was no longer conscious of the ache in his left side, or of the nausea. Part of the pattern that had been trying to form in his mind for hours took firm, clear shape. Hunt was looking at him expectantly, waiting for a comment. "That's interesting," Chee said.

"It is," Hunt agreed. "We never could figure it

out. Obviously the bomb wasn't intended for the wrecker crew—although we finally even checked on that. You'd figure if a guy puts a bomb in a pickup, he wants to waste the pickup driver. But the driver was a poor-boy Navajo who was already on his last legs with cancer. Already dying. No motive to hurry it along. Then we checked on the guy who had the parking space reserved. Big shot doctor. Money. Wife trouble. Maybe she wanted an instant divorce. No evidence, but we figured the doctor was the target. Now it looks like we got our bomber killing another Navajo, and he's got the same last name."

"They're father and son," Chee said.

Hunt slapped his leg. "That's exactly what I hoped you'd say. That, or maybe brothers. You know for sure?"

"I know it for sure," Chee said.

"Well, now," Hunt said. "That tells us a couple of things."

Yes, Chee was thinking. It should tell us a lot. But he couldn't think of what.

"Like what?" he asked.

"Like that bomb wasn't intended for the doctor. If that hit man was aiming for Charley Junior, he must have been aiming for Charley Senior."

"Yes," Chee said. His head ached. Who would hire a professional killer to murder a man who was already dying? Why would anyone want to hurry the death of Emerson Charley? There were no apparent answers. Hunt was watching Chee, waiting for more response.

"Did Emerson Charley's body ever turn up?"

Hunt frowned. "What do you mean?"

"Tomas Charley told me that the hospital lost his daddy's body. Emerson died one night, and Tomas came to get the body the next morning, and it was gone out of the morgue."

Hunt opened his mouth, and closed it again. "I didn't know that," he said. "Be damned. Why wasn't it reported?"

"Tomas reported it to APD," Chee said.

Hunt's embarrassment showed. "You know how that'd be," he said. "Probably told some clerk at the front desk, and filled in a form, and somebody did a little calling around, and that was about it. Nobody pushing it. By then the bombing case wasn't active. And nobody up front would have a way to know the detective division was interested in a sick Navajo."

"Guess not," Chee said.

"I'll check on it. Right away." He frowned again. "How can a hospital lose a body?"

"Tomas thinks it was stolen."

"Stolen? Why? Who'd steal it? This guy?" He tapped the drawing.

Chee didn't feel like talking about the Vineses. "Tomas thinks a witch stole it," he said. "Why? Who knows?" But a reason was forming in his mind.

And, apparently, in the mind of Hunt.

"What did he die of?" Hunt asked. "They told us he had cancer."

"But maybe the guy who tried to hurry him along with the bomb found another way to hurry him along. That's what you're thinking?" Chee found himself respecting the way Hunt's mind worked, and liking the man.

"Exactly," Hunt said. "And if the body's gone, there's no autopsy. I'll check into that."

"Good," Chee said.

"I'll let you know," Hunt said. "And there's one other thing." He fished the sketch out of the folder again and looked at it. "If our man here is the same as your man, I think he's a biggie. I think the FBI's going to be very interested."

"They were here this morning," Chee said. "The nurse wouldn't let 'em in. What do they want?"

"Past several years they've had a run of professional killings done a lot the same. People shot in the head with a .22. Nobody hears a shot. And then there was a couple of cases where they had one person hit with a .22 and one bombed. A couple of hoods in the construction union in Houston and witnesses in an extortion case in Philadelphia. Anyway, mostly the little silenced pistol and a couple of times with the bomb. And both times the bombs seem to have been the kind that get set off by tilting the package. That's the kind of bomb he used here."

"Tilting the package?"

"Clever as hell," Hunt said. "It uses mercury to make the electrical connection. You just set the damn thing down and take off the safety gadget, and the next time the thing moves, or tilts, or shakes, the mercury slides and it goes off. No timer to screw you up, no wiring it up to the ignition. No fuss. No muss.

If the driver doesn't see it, it goes off when the car moves. If he does see it, it goes off when he picks it up."

"Then what went wrong here?" Chee asked.

"Luck. Wrecker crew was going to haul off the truck," Hunt said. "They started to hoist the rear end. Tilt. Boom. But that was sheer bad luck. It's quite a gadget. Understand the CIA developed it."

The FBI arrived as Hunt was leaving. His name was Martin. He was young. He wore a brown suit with a vest. His mustache was trim, and his haircut would not have offended the late J. Edgar Hoover. Being second to an Albuquerque policeman did not please him.

"The nurse told me you were asleep," he said. It was more an accusation than a statement.

"No," Chee said. "I was watching *Hollywood Squares*. I guess she didn't want to interrupt. Ever watch 'em?"

Martin denied it. He wanted to talk about what the blond man looked like. And about why anyone would want Tomas Charley killed. And about the Vines burglary. It took Chee less than five minutes to exhaust all he knew about all three subjects and ten minutes more to go over it all twice more from slightly different angles.

"You find anything in the man's car?" Chee asked. "It was a rental car, wasn't it?"

"We haven't recovered it yet," Martin said. "We think it was rented from Hertz at the Albuquerque airport." He fished a folder from his briefcase and extracted a copy of Hunt's sketch.

"Your man look like this?"

"Pretty close," Chee said.

"The Hertz people identified him as the man who rented a green-and-white Plymouth sedan. Now the car's overdue. He gave his name as McRae and an Indiana address. It doesn't check out."

Chee didn't comment. Talking to Hunt had tired him. His chest hurt. His ears were ringing. He wanted Martin to go away.

"When you get out of here, we want you to come down to the office," Martin said. "We want you to look at mug shots and give us more details on the identification if you can."

"Mug shots? You think you have a record on him?"

"Not really," Martin said. "We think we have a ten-year accumulation of suspicions. We want you to look just in case. And we want you to spend a lot of time remembering everything you can about him. Everything."

Chee said nothing. He just closed his eyes.

"It's important," Martin said. "This guy's slick. That little pistol he used must be really silent. And he gets it in places where nobody sees anything. Apparently he scouts everything out very methodically, and then he likes to catch them alone for one quick close shot at the head. In the john is a favorite of his. We know of four found sitting on the john with the stall door closed. And a couple in telephone booths. Places like that. A quick shot and he just walks away. Never any witnesses. Not until the bombing. And now you and Miss Landon."

Chee opened his eyes. "We're the first witnesses?"

Martin was staring at him. "The first he knows about. He didn't know anyone saw him putting the bomb in Charley's truck. Medium-sized. Blond. So forth. You're the only two who actually got a look at him and who could pin him to a killing."

Chee's head ached. He closed his eyes again.

"You know," Martin said, "I think I'd be careful if I were you."

Chee had already had that thought.

16

WHEN MARTIN LEFT, Chee spent the next ten minutes on the telephone. He got Mary Landon's number from information, but no one answered when he called it. He remembered then that it was a school day and called the school. Miss Landon had taken the day off. He called his own office, explained the situation, and told Officer Dodge to see if she could find Mary and do what she could do to keep an eye on her. The doctor came in then—a young man with red hair and freckles. He inspected Chee's ribs, replaced the dressing, said, "Take it easy," and left. The nurse arrived, took his temperature, gave him two pills, watched while he took them, said, "This isn't a police station. You're supposed to be resting," and left. Chee rearranged himself on the pillow and gazed out across the university campus. He thought about Mary, and about the peyote religion, and B. J. Vines' keepsake box, and the ways of white men, and drifted off into an uneasy sleep. When he awoke it was late afternoon. The sun was slanting through his window and Mary sat in the bedside chair.

"Hello," she said. "How're you feeling?"

"Fine," Chee said. He did feel fine. Vastly relieved.

"Boy," she said. "You sure scared me. I thought you were dead. I waved down a truck, and he got that state policeman on his CB radio. And when we got back to you, you were just lying there." She grimaced at him. "Like dead."

Chee told her what he'd learned about the blond man. "You see the problem? There's a chance he's going to decide he needs to get rid of us."

Even as he was saying them, the words sounded melodramatic to him. In this quiet, antiseptic room, the idea of anyone wanting to kill Jim Chee and Mary Landon seemed foolish.

"Don't you think what he'd really do is just run?" Mary asked. "That's what I'd do."

"But you're not a professional gunman," Chee said.

"If that remark's a reflection on my shooting, I want to remind you that it was you who screwed up the rear sight."

"Be serious," Chee said. "This guy kills people."

The humor left Mary's face. "I know," she said. "But what can you do? It's sort of like being struck by lightning. You can't go around all the time hiding from clouds."

"But you don't stand under trees while it's raining, either," Chee said. "Why don't you take a leave and go off and visit some relatives somewhere for a while and don't tell anyone where you're going?"

Mary's expression shifted from somber to skeptical. "Is that what you're going to do?"

"I would if I could," Chee said. "But I'm a policeman. It's my business."

"No, it's not," Mary said. "You don't even have jurisdiction. That's what you told me. It's FBI business. Or maybe the sheriff's."

"Legally," Chee said. "But this sore rib sort of gives me a special interest. And besides, I'm a material witness."

"So am I," Mary said.

They argued about it, an uneasy, tentative sparring of two persons not yet sure of their relationship.

Mary changed the subject to his earlier visitors, to Sheriff Sena, to Sena's obsession with the death of his brother in the oil well explosion. The conversation was oddly strained and uncomfortable.

"When I get out of here," Chee said, "I'm going to dig into the newspaper files and learn everything I can about that oil well accident, and get some names, and see what I can find out."

"I'll go see about it," Mary said. "The university library keeps newspapers on microfilm." She got up and collected her purse. "I'll see if they have the right ones. If I hurry, I can get it done today."

17

IT WAS 3:11 A.M. when Chee looked at his watch. He had been awake perhaps fifteen minutes, lying motionless with his eyes closed in the vain hope that sleep would return. Now he gave it up. Sleeping away the afternoon had left him out of tune with time. The nurse had given him another sleeping pill at ten o'clock but he had let it lay. His policy was to take pills only when unavoidable. Having his sleeping habits dislocated was the price he was now paying for that pill at lunch. He sat on the edge of the bed and put on the hospital slippers. Much of the soreness had gone out of his side. Only when he moved was there still pain under the heavy bandages. Through the curtain that now partitioned the room he could hear the heavy breathing of a drugged sleep. They had wheeled a man in from the post-surgery recovery room about midnight—a young Chicano sewn up after some sort of accident earlier in the evening. Chee flicked on his bed light and began to reread the newspaper. Through the curtain he heard his roommate mumble in his sleep. The man shifted his position, groaned. Chee switched off the light. Let him sleep, he thought. This is the time of night for sleeping. But Chee had never felt more wide awake. He put on his robe and walked down to the nurse's station. The nurse was a woman in her middle forties, with a round, placid face and a complexion marred by those ten thousand wrinkles the desert sun inflicts upon white people. She glanced up from her paperwork through bifocal glasses.

"Can't sleep," Chee said.

"Let's see," Bifocals said. "You're Chee?" She found his folder and glanced at it. "You had a pill at ten, but I guess I could give you another one."

"I don't like 'em," Chee said. "They make me drowsy."

Bifocals gave him a double take, detected the irony, and grinned. "Yes," she said. "That's the trouble with sleeping pills."

"A while back this hospital lost a body," Chee said. "Fellow named Emerson Charley. You hear about that?"

"Not officially," Bifocals said. "But I heard." She grinned at the memory. "There was some hell raised over it."

"How could it happen? What do you do with bodies?"

"Well, first the attending physician comes, takes care of the certification," Bifocals said. She looked thoughtful. "Then the body is tagged for identification and moved to the morgue on the second floor.

It's held there until relatives get a funeral home to claim it. Or, if there's an autopsy, it's tagged for that, and it's held until the morphology laboratory does the postmortem. The way I heard about this one, it was tagged for an autopsy, but somebody came and took it."

"Tell me about it," Chee said.

"Nothing to tell. He died late in the day. The body was taken down and put in the cooler. In the morning, morphology called for it and the body was gone." Bifocals grinned. "Lots of embarrassment. Lots of red faces."

"Did somebody steal the body?"

"Had to be that," Bifocals said. "Somebody in the family, probably. Indians usually don't want an autopsy made."

Chee didn't correct her. Charley was a Navajo and most Navajos had even less distaste for autopsies than do whites. It was the Pueblo Indians who tended to resist autopsies. Their dead needed to be buried in the same cycle of the sun as their death. They had to begin on time the tightly scheduled four-day journey of the soul into eternity. But for most of the Navajo clans, death produced only a short-lived and evil ghost, and everlasting oblivion for the human consciousness. They had little sentiment for corpses.

"Could somebody just walk in and walk out with a body?" Chee asked.

"I guess they did," Bifocals said. "And with clothing, too." She chuckled. "We had two flaps out of this one. First the body was missing, and then two days later it turned out we'd given this Emerson Charley's clothing to another corpse. Whoever took him took the other man's clothing."

"How could that happen?"

"Easy enough. When a patient comes in, his clothing goes into a red plastic bag—looks sort of like a shopping bag—and it goes to the morgue with the body. Whoever got the body just picked up the wrong bag."

"But don't they keep the place locked?"

"Supposed to be. But somebody probably left it open for some funeral home. That's what I think happened. And somebody from the man's family came, found it unlocked, and just walked out with the body. The morgue's right by the laundry dock. They could go out that way and nobody would see them. And you should be back in bed."

"Okay," Chee said. "Good night."

But Chee still wasn't sleepy. At his doorway, he glanced back. Bifocals was immersed in her paperwork. He walked down the hall, around the corner, and out the door to the elevator landing. He took the stairway down to second, and paused there to get his directions. From what Bifocals said, the morgue was near the laundry loading dock. That made sense in terms of logistics. The hospital was built on a slope, a hillside that angled downward from northeast to southwest. Thus if the laundry loading dock was on a second floor, it must be on the northeast side of the hospital. Chee took a hall that led north and made a right turn eastward. As he walked down this empty, echoing corridor he could hear thumping sounds ahead. The sounds, Chee guessed, a laundry would make. On the next door, a sheet of typing paper had been stuck. A legend printed on it with a marking pen declared that the morphology laboratory had been moved to the New Mexico State Laboratory. Just around the corner, Chee found the door to the morgue. It was a wide door, protected by a plywood bumper sheet. Three body-tables-on-wheels were parked beside it. The door was locked. Chee examined the lock. He guessed he could open it with a flexible blade, but there was no way to be sure. The ceiling offered another possibility. He glanced up and down the hallway and down the connecting hall that led to the laundry dock. All deserted. The only sound was the thumping of the laundry machinery. Chee pushed one of the carts against the door and climbed stiffly atop it. He lifted the acoustical ceiling tile and stuck his head through the opening. There was about four feet of crawl space between the false ceiling and the floor above. Chee tested the aluminum-alloy gridwork that supported the ceiling tiles. It seemed sturdy but probably not strong enough to support the full weight of a man. There were, however, other means of support—electrical-cable conduits, water pipes, and the heavily insulated sheet-metal tubes through which the hot and cold air of the heating-cooling system flowed. Chee could see well enough in the darkness now to tell that getting into the morgue wouldn't be difficult even if the door was locked. One could simply climb into the false ceiling, cross the partition, lift another of the acoustical tiles, and drop into the room. He withdrew his head, and sliding the ceiling section back into place, climbed gingerly down from the body cart. At the elevator he yawned. Suddenly he felt both tired and relaxed. He had answered a question that no one had asked, and that didn't matter anyway. But now he could sleep.

18

COLTON WOLF HAD LEFT the car parked in
the darkness about fifty yards from the laundry loading dock. He tested the dock entrance door. It was
unlocked. Then he circled the hospital, checking the
parking lots. He found no police cars. His plan was
simple. He would use the front entrance of the hospital. He would take the stairs to the fifth-floor postsurgical wing, find room 572, and kill the Indian
policeman. The next steps would depend on the circumstances—whether there was any sort of disturbance. Colton expected none. The Indian policeman
would be sleeping the heavy sleep that hospitals im-
pose upon their patients. He should present no problem. If there was a nurse on duty, Colton would
evade her if he could and kill her quietly if he
couldn't. And then he would walk downstairs, take
the hall past the morgue, go out the laundry loading
dock exit, and drive away in a common, nondescript
two-year-old Chevy. He had taken the Chevy from
the low-rate, long-term parking lot at the airport;

the ticket on the dashboard of the one he picked showed it had already been left overnight. It might not be missed for days. But in the event it was missed, he had stopped in the parking lot of an all-night grocery store and switched license plates.

It was cold. Colton hated cold. He felt exposed and vulnerable. Overhead, as he walked across the almost empty front-entrance parking lot, the sky was a dazzle of strange stars. Unlike the soft, warm protecting darkness of his California boyhood, the night here was hostile. He could hear the soft sound of his crepe-rubber soles on the asphalt, the sound of his trouser legs rubbing, cloth on cloth. Behind him a truck moved up Lomas Avenue. Except for that, the night was silent. Colton squeezed the pistol in his coat pocket. It had a solid, reassuring feel. It was a good piece. Long-barreled and unhandy to look at, but efficient. He had made most of it himself to exactly fit his needs. The grip was walnut, roughed to eliminate the possibility of fingerprints, as was every metal surface. The barrel was threaded at both ends so that a half turn removed the silencer from its muzzle and a turn and a half detached barrel from firing chamber. Only the barrel—with its telltale ballistic tracks left on the lethal bullet—was directly incriminating Within minutes after a job, the barrel was disposed of and a new barrel screwed into place—apparent proof that the pistol Colton carried had never been fired.

The automatic door sighed open in front of him and closed behind him. Inside, the air was stuffy. The young woman at the reception desk was reading what looked like a textbook. She didn't glance at Colton. From somewhere out of sight down a hallway came the sound of a cart being pushed. No problems. Colton adjusted his plans. He walked past the stairwell door to the elevators. Entering a lift, he pushed the sixth-floor button. The elevator rose silently, a new machine in a new wing. Colton took out the pistol, quickly checked the round in the chamber and the cocking mechanism. Perfect. Some would have said the caliber was too small for killing humans. A .22, they would say, was for rabbits. But Colton believed in silence. With a silencer on, a .22 made no more sound than a finger makes thumping on a skull. Small but sufficient, and for Colton's purposes, it was perfect. He had studied the skull and the brain within it in the Baylor University library when he was living in Waco. He understood the skull's bone thickness, and the tissue forms behind the bone, and where a small lead pellet could be placed above the hairline so that it would kill instantly and inevitably.

Colton put his hand, with the pistol gripped in it, back into his coat pocket before the elevator stopped at the sixth floor. The door slid open. He listened. He moved to the front of the elevator, pushed the door hold button, and listened again. Nothing. No one was in the hall. He walked to the stairwell door and moved quietly downward.

The policeman's name was Jimmy Chee. The newspaper said he had suffered a bullet wound in the chest and had undergone surgery. The woman with him was named Mary Landon, a schoolteacher at Crownpoint elementary school. The woman could wait. She had not seen him as closely as had the policeman. The policeman had stared at him at the rug auction, and policemen were trained to remember faces. At the bottom of the stairs, Colton reviewed his plan.

Room 572 was a double room. At 6:00 P.M., when Colton had called to ask about Chee, the nurse had said he had no roommate. Probably he would still be alone. That would make it simpler. A roommate would probably not awaken. If he did awaken, his bed would doubtless be screened from the target's bed. Keep the killing to an absolute minimum, that was Colton's rule. The less killing, the shorter the manhunt it provoked.

Colton paused just inside the stairwell door, listening again. Here was a crucial point. With a policeman wounded under these circumstances, there was a chance a guard would be posted. This was why Colton hadn't risked arriving in an elevator. He peered through the glass panel of the stairwell door. No one visible. He slipped silently out of the stairwell to the ward door. He listened again. Nothing. Things had gone perfectly so far. Now the risk must be taken.

He pushed through the swinging doors. A nurse was walking directly toward him. She was a medium-sized woman, perhaps forty-five, with dark hair covered by a nursing cap. Behind horn-rimmed glasses, her face registered surprise. "Yes?" she said.

"I'm Dr. Duncan," Colton Wolf said. "You have a patient named Jimmy Chee. I think we have him down for the wrong medication." He said it without hesitation, walking directly toward the nursing station, where the charts would be kept. Dealing with the nurse was the sort of contingency Colton was always prepared for. There was no guard in sight. But one might be sitting in the room with Chee.

"I think it's just a broad-spectrum antibiotic and a pain-killer," the nurse said.

"Let's take a look," Colton said. "I heard they were going to have a guard up here for one of the patients. What's the story?"

"Nobody told me anything about it," the nurse said. Behind the nursing station desk, she flipped quickly through the medication order slips. "I'm almost sure it was Achromycin and Empirin number three," she said, intent on the forms. "Who wanted it changed?"

"The surgeon," Colton said. He extracted the pistol, cocking it as it left his pocket. He raised it, muzzle a half inch from the tip of the white cap.

"Here it is," she said. "Let's see . . ."

Colton squeezed the trigger. The pistol thumped and produced a thin spurt of blue smoke. The nurse's head fell forward onto the desktop. Colton held her with his free left hand on her shoulder until he was sure she wouldn't slip from the chair. Then he felt under her ear. The pulse fluttered, and fluttered, and died. If anyone looked in, the nurse appeared to be asleep at her desk. Now he would find room 572, finish the policeman, and leave.

19

JIM CHEE HAD BEEN in the bathroom, getting himself a pre-bed drink. Then, from the doorway, he had watched the nurse get up from her desk and walk toward the swinging doors. He had seen them open, and the man enter. The man wore a blue cotton hospital coat. He was blond, with pale skin and pale-blue eyes, and Chee recognized him instantly. The recognition was a two-staged affair. First came the thought that he had seen the blond doctor now walking toward him at the Crownpoint rug auction; a millisecond later came the gut-wrenching realization that the blond doctor was the man who had killed Tomas Charley and was no doctor at all but had come here to kill him. Chee stepped back from the doorway. He felt a desperate panic. The window! It didn't open, and it led to nothing but a lethal drop. The man was between him and the only exit from the wing. Chee forced himself to think. A weapon? There was nothing that would work against this marksman's pistol. Could he hide?

He swung himself quickly onto the bed and stood pushing the acoustical tile overhead. The space here was like that on the second floor, and here, too, the space between the false ceiling and the floor above was crisscrossed with electrical wiring, pipes, and the rectangular sheet-metal conduits that carried hot and cold air. Chee had no time to check weight-carrying capacity. He pushed the tile aside, grasped the brace that held the air-return conduit, and pulled himself painfully into the ceiling space.

The conduit was perhaps two feet wide and wrapped in a white insulation material. Chee maneuvered himself on top of it, reached frantically back, and pushed the tile into place. He found he was panting, partly from the sudden violent exertion and partly, he guessed, from fear. He controlled his breathing. Even with the tiles pushed back into place, the darkness was not absolute. He lay face down on the conduit insulation, smelling dust. He could hear the sounds buildings make at night, a ticking from somewhere in the darkness to his left, the noise of the elevator motor, and a faint hiss which might be nothing more than air passing through the metal tube under his ear. There were no voices. The conversation between the blond man and the nurse had stopped. Chee raised his head and stared down the conduit into the darkness. If he crawled along it, it would take him over the elevator foyer. But could he reach it without noise? The conduit braces supported it about six inches above the ceiling tiles, which left about two feet of space above it—enough for crawling but not enough for any rapid hands-and-knees scrambling. Chee gripped the insulation and pulled himself cautiously forward. The movement was almost soundless, but it turned the throbbing pain in his ribs to a sharp dagger thrust of agony. He suppressed his gasp by holding his breath. As he released it, he heard a metallic noise just below him.

Chee recognized the sound. It was made when the curtain that surrounded the beds was pulled along its metal track. The man who had come to kill him was standing just below. Only a quarter inch of Celotex insulation and perhaps forty-eight inches of air separated him from the blond man and his pistol. Chee lay utterly still. What would the blond man do? Would he think of the hollow ceiling as a hiding place? Chee turned his thoughts away from that. What was that blond man doing now? Chee imagined him standing, pistol ready, staring with those patient, incurious eyes at Chee's empty bed. He would look behind the bed, and in the bathroom, and behind the curtain that surrounded the bed of Chee's roommate. With that thought another came. Would the blond man mistake the Chicano for a Navajo? He might. The realization brought two contradictory emotions. Pity for the man sleeping a drugged postsurgical sleep below him struggled with a desperate hunger to stay alive.

Something bumped against metal. Then silence. Then a creaking noise. Silence again. His rib stabbed him with pain, and his lungs cried out for air. The curtain rustled. What should he do? What could he do?

Then there was another sound. A thump. A knuckle whacked against wood? And then a sort of sigh and a rasping intake of breath. Silence again, followed finally by the whisper of soft soles on a polished floor. The room door clicked shut.

Chee took in some air as quietly as he could. Relief flooded through him. He felt himself shaking. The man had gone. Not far, perhaps. Perhaps only to check other rooms. Perhaps he would be back. But at least for the moment, death had walked away. Perhaps the blond man wouldn't come back. Perhaps Chee would live. He felt a kind of crazy joy. He would wait. He would lie there motionless forever—until morning came, until he heard the voice of a nurse below him, arriving with his morning medicine. He would take no chance at all that the blond man was waiting somewhere for him to move.

Chee waited, and listened. He heard absolutely nothing but the natural sounds of the night. Time ticked away. Perhaps three minutes. Chee became aware of an odor. It was acrid—faint but unmistakable. The smell of gun smoke. What could have caused it? He knew the answer almost instantly. The thumping sound had been a shot from the blond man's pistol.

Chee reached down from the conduit, carefully moved a ceiling tile aside, and looked down. To eyes adjusted to darkness above the ceiling, the room was comparatively bright. He could see only his bed and an expanse of floor beside it. He gripped the conduit braces and lowered himself. The blond man was gone. Chee pulled back the curtain by his roommate's bed. The man's dark head lay on the pillow, neatly, face toward the ceiling, eyes closed in the profound sleep that follows surgery. But behind the curtain the smell of smoke was stronger. Chee reached out a tentative hand. He touched the sleeping face. His forefinger rested just under the nose. His fingertip felt warm skin. But there was no breath. He moved his hand downward, letting the palm rest over the sheet against the chest, holding it there. The man's face, illuminated dimly by the city night through the window, was young and clean-shaven, a longish face with a slightly sardonic cast. Chee had been training himself away from seeing all non-Navajos as looking very much alike. This one looked mostly Spanish in blood, with a little Pueblo Indian. The chest under Chee's palm moved not at all. No lung stirred, no heartbeat. The mouth Chee saw was a dead mouth. He shifted his eyes away from it and looked for a moment out into the night. Then he walked quickly to the door and pulled it open. There was no fear now. He ran to the nurse's station and picked up the telephone beside the hand of the sleeping nurse, and dialed past the switchboard to the Albuquerque Police Department's number.

While he talked, quickly describing the deed, the man, and the pistol, and suggesting that the gunman was probably in a new green-and-white Plymouth sedan, his free hand touched the hair of the nurse, felt the cap, and found the small round hole burned in the crest of it.

"Make it two homicides," Chee said. "He also shot the fifth-floor nurse."

20

EVEN AS HE TROTTED down the stairs toward the laundry level something troubled Colton Wolf about the policeman's room. Why was the unused bed rumpled? Had a visitor sprawled on it? It seemed too unkempt for that. But there was something else out of tune. He had left the loading dock and was walking toward the car he was using when he realized what it was. The smell around the face of the man he had shot was an anesthetic. Natural enough. But it was too strong. It was still being exhaled. Chee had been out of surgery far too long to smell like that.

"Son of a bitch!" Colton said. He ran back to the loading dock and was through the door before his caution stopped him. How had Chee escaped? Where was he now? He would have called for help. Certainly he'd be alert. And Chee was a very smart cop—that was clear. A second try now would be too risky. There wasn't time.

He was out of the parking lot and heading westward on Lomas Avenue when he heard the first siren. But he wasn't worried. No one had seen the car. He left it three blocks from where he had stolen it, walked to his pickup, and drove slowly back to his trailer. By the time he had reached it, his new plan for killing Jimmy Chee was taking shape. It was a good plan. This time Chee wouldn't escape.

21

CHEE KEPT the control lever of the viewer pressed halfway to the right. Above his forehead, the microfilm reels hummed. The pages of the *Grants Daily Beacon* fled past his eyes like the boxcars of a freight passing a traffic signal. They moved too fast to be read, but not too fast to tell a front page from a grocery ad, or to spot the sort of black banner headline that would signal the kind of story he was looking for. Half of Chee's attention focused on the moving image under his eyes. But he was aware of the silence of this huge basement room in Zimmerman Library, of the new .38 caliber revolver that weighted his coat pocket, and of Hunt pretending to be studying beyond the glass pane of the carrel door behind him. He was also aware of the nearness of Mary Landon.

The page that flashed below his eyes had a heavy black streak across the top. He stopped the reel and pushed the lever to the left to back it up. The headline read:

"Ha!" Mary Landon said. "Wrong disaster." She was sitting beside and a little behind him, saying nothing much. She brought to his sensitive nostrils the scent of clothing dried in sunlight, and of soap.

Chee pushed the lever to the right again and glanced up. A librarian moved down the aisle to his left, pushing a cart loaded with bound periodicals. A slender white girl with a fur-collared coat was hunting something in the microfilm files. Beyond her, movement caught Chee's eye. An elbow, covered with blue nylon, jutted out from behind one of the square white pillars. It retracted, jutted out again, retracted, jutted. Doing what? Someone scratching himself?

Chee wanted suddenly to look over his shoulder, to make sure that Hunt was still in the carrel, alert and ready. He resisted the urge. Theoretically, Hunt was tagging along as a guard. But while it hadn't exactly been spoken, it was understood that purpose number one was to get the blond man. Protecting Chee was a by-product. It sounded cold-blooded but it made sense. One protected Chee and Mary Landon by catching the blond man. There was no other way to do it. The law wanted very, very badly to catch the blond man. On the other hand, the world was full of tribal policemen.

Under his eyes, the record of June 1948 raced past and became July. The reels overhead hummed, paused, hummed again, paused again. On this pause the banner read:

WELL EXPLOSION KILLS CREW

"Here it is," Chee said.
The subhead added:

TWELVE FEARED DEAD
IN BLAST ON RIG FLOOR

"Scoot over a little," Mary said. She leaned over the projected page, pressed against him, reminding him again of sunshine and soap.

All members of an oil well drilling crew were apparently killed instantly northwest of Grants several days ago in what authorities believe to have been the premature explosion of a nitroglycerin charge.

Valencia County Sheriff Gilberto Garcia said the toll may be as high as twelve men, including ten working on the drilling crew on the east slope of Mount Taylor and two employees of the oil field supply company, who had brought in the nitro charge.

Garcia said the death toll is uncertain because the force of the blast "blew everything apart and scattered bits and pieces of people for half a mile."

"It looks like they had the nitro on the floor of the well when it went off," Garcia said. "It didn't leave much." He said the explosion probably took place Friday, which was the day the crew from Petrolab, Inc., delivered the explosive to the site. The accident was not discovered until Monday, when a deputy sheriff went to the site to investigate why men working there had not been heard from.

Garcia said the well is about 25 miles north and west of Grants near the border of the Checkerboard district of the Navajo reservation. "We haven't found anyone who heard the explosion," the sheriff said. "No one lives for miles around out there."

The sheriff said coyotes, other predators, and scavenger birds had complicated the problem of identifications. "We think we have one identification positive now, and we expect we have enough to pin down a couple of others, but we're not too optimistic about the rest."

He said payroll records named the drilling crew as Nelson Kirby, about 40, of Sherman, Texas, the crew chief; Albert Novitski, age and address unknown; Carl Lebeck, age unknown, a geologist who was logging the well; Robert Sena, 24, of Grants, and six as yet unidentified Navajos working on the well as a roustabout crew.

Also feared killed were R. J. Mackensen, about 60, and Theo Roff, about 20, both employees of Petrolab, a Farmington company which supplied the explosive.

Chee scanned the remaining paragraphs.

"Pretty much what Sena told you?" Mary asked. "The names ring any bells?"

"Just Robert Sena," Chee said. "He was Gordo's big brother."

Mary was reading over his shoulder. "Carl Lebeck," she said. "My cousin used to date a boy named Carl Lebeck. Or maybe it was Le Bow. Something like that."

"Let's see what they said when they found the Navajos were alive," Chee said.

It was on the front page of the Wednesday edition, a brief item reporting that the crew of six Navajo laborers, originally believed killed in the explosion, hadn't gone to work that day. The story included their names, which Chee copied off in his notebook. It didn't mention why they had missed work. Chee found that in the following day's paper. Again the headline stretched black across the top of the page:

ARREST MADE IN WELL BLAST

SHERIFF REPORTS NAVAJOS
GIVEN ADVANCE TIP

One of the Navajo workers who escaped last week's fatal explosion at a Valencia County oil drilling site was being questioned today about reports that he had advance knowledge the explosion would occur.

Sheriff Gilberto Garcia identified the man as Dillon Charley. He said Charley has admitted warning five other Navajo co-workers at the well not to go to work last Friday "because something bad was going to happen."

"He claims he got the warning from God in

some sort of religious vision," Garcia said. He said that Charley is the "peyote chief" in the Native American cult and that the five other Navajos on the work crew were also members of the religious organization.

Members of the cult chew seed buttons from the peyote cactus as part of their rites. A narcotic in the peyote reportedly affects the nervous system, causing hallucinations in some users. Possession of the substance is illegal, and the Navajo Tribal Council has passed specific legislation banning its use or possession on the reservation.

The sheriff also revealed that Charley had been injured in what Garcia called "an attempt to resist arrest." He said Deputy Sheriff Lawrence Sena had been placed under suspension "until we can determine if undue force was used." Deputy Sena's brother, Robert Sena, was one of the men blown to bits when a nitroglycerin charge went off prematurely at the well last Friday.

"Notice that?" Chee asked. He poked his finger at the proper paragraph. "Gordo roughed up Dillon Charley. He must have *really* roughed him up to get suspended for it. Beating up a Navajo wasn't considered such a big deal in those days." He leaned back, away from the microfilm projector hood, and looked at Mary. Her expression was quizzical.

"What do you think?" he asked.

"I think you're strange," she said. "I think you're weird. You have this creepy murderer trying to shoot you, and you're down here all excited, reading about something that happened thirty years ago."

"You, too," Chee said. "How about you?"

"I'm not excited," she said.

"I mean he's trying to shoot you, too."

"I don't believe that," Mary said. "You're the one who got a good look at him. You're the one he came after." She looked away from him, leaning again into the microfilm reader. A nice profile, Chee thought. Nice. She was looking down, reading the projected type. Her eyes were very blue and the lashes curved away from them in a long, graceful sweep. Her hair fell across her cheek. Soft hair. Soft cheek.

"Another thing," Mary said without glancing up. "What's all this concern about a cop beating up a Navajo? From what I heard at Laguna, the worst cops for beating up Navajos were Navajo cops."

"We'd rather beat up Anglos," Chee said, "but we don't have jurisdiction over you folks." He watched her profile as he said it, looking for the reaction that would tell him something about her. Her jibe about Navajo police was partly serious—probably mostly serious. Navajo police, like most police, had a reputation of being toughest on their own people. Her eyes were still on the projected page. "You haven't really told me what happened up in the hospital. How you got away. And you haven't told me your secret name."

The elbow had reappeared from behind the pillar. Motionless now. Its owner must be leaning on the pillar. Reading, perhaps.

"I hid," Chee said. "Like a rabbit."

She looked at him. "Why like a rabbit? You think you should have come on like Monster Slayer?" She grabbed his wrist and raised his hand. "Me mighty redskin. Me take on gun with bare hands. Me big hero. Me dead, but me hero." She dropped his hand. "If you didn't have time to do a little ghost dance to make your hospital gown bulletproof, I think the smart thing to do was get under the bed."

"The way it worked, I guess I was hiding behind another guy. My roommate." He gave her a quick sketch of what had happened, from the furtive trip downstairs to find out how the body had been stolen from the morgue. He told it quickly, without interpretation and without speculation. Just the facts, he thought. Just the facts. And while he told them, he watched her face.

She pursed her lips into a soundless whistle and shuddered. "I'd have been terrified." She looked at him a moment, her lower lip caught between her teeth. "How did you think to climb up into the ceiling?"

"That's not the point," Chee said. "The point is I got away because I left the blond man somebody to shoot. He came into the room to shoot himself an Indian. Nobody home but a Mexican. So the Chicano gets shot instead of me."

She was frowning at him again. "So?"

"So? What do you mean, so?"

"So what," she said. "You on some guilt trip? You think you should have stayed behind? Bared your chest and said, 'Here I am. Don't shoot this other guy.' Come *on.*" Her voice was scornful. "He shot the nurse, didn't he? The only difference would have been he'd have shot both of you."

"Maybe," Chee said.

"You really are weird," Mary Landon said. "Either that, or you want me to think you are."

"Well," Chee said. "No use talking about it now. Let's see what else we can find."

They found very little. There was a lengthy story about the Native American Church, the ceremony, and what the members said about Dillon Charley's vision of warning. There was a short item in which the sheriff reported that one of the victims had been definitely identified from dental work as an employee of Petrolab. But the story seemed quickly to die away for lack of new information.

If Sena, or any of the other victims, was identified, it wasn't mentioned in the *Beacon.* Nor was there any follow-up story on the arrest of Dillon Charley. His release, whenever it happened, went without notice in the paper.

They worked through the microfilm slowly now, page by page, looking for the remainders of a story that was no longer banner headline news. Halfway through the September editions, after an hour of finding nothing, Mary had an idea.

"Hey," she said. "Newspapers do anniversary stories. You know. They start, 'A year ago today . . .' and then they rehash it all. Why don't we skip ahead a year?"

Chee stood and stretched. He pushed the lever to

the left. The reels hummed with the rewinding. The young woman had left the microfilm area. The elbow was missing from the pillar. Protruding now into Chee's line of vision was the tip of a nose and a shock of hair. The hair was blond. Very blond. Chee felt his stomach muscles tighten. He released the lever and moved his right hand into his coat pocket. The hand found the pistol grip. The thumb found the hammer.

"What?" Mary said. She was staring at him.

The man emerged from behind the pillar. He glanced at Mary. He was very blond, but he wasn't the blond man. Far too young. No resemblance at all. He moved to the microfilm file and began rummaging.

"Nothing," Chee said. "I'm just jumpy."

They found the anniversary story. It reported little new.

By the time the copying desk had made Xeroxes of the microfilmed stories for them, it was five o'-clock.

"Now what?" Mary asked. "It occurs to me that Sergeant Chee of the Mounties has just wasted one afternoon, plus the afternoon of one Crownpoint schoolteacher, and isn't going to have the slightest idea of what to do next. This is a dead end. Right?"

"No," Chee said. They were climbing the stairway that spiraled upward through the four levels of the working end of the university library. An artist had used the stairwell walls to depict in paint and plaster the history of man's efforts to record his communication with his fellows. Here, below the ground floor, they climbed past pictographs and petroglyphs. The Phoenician alphabet was far overhead, and the symbolic language of computers even higher. "Maybe it doesn't lead anywhere, but I'd like to talk to some of those men who got warned away from that explosion. I'd like to find out what Dillon Charley told them."

They emerged on the ground-floor level. Through the glass south wall of the library, the Humanities Building loomed above the sycamores of the central mall, a monolithic sculpture against a dark-blue autumn sky. Usually Chee liked the building. Today it reminded him of tombstones.

"Why?" Mary said. "What can they possibly tell you that has anything to do with this?"

"Maybe nothing," Chee said. "But the killings grew out of the keepsake box, and stealing the keepsake box seems to have something to do somehow with Dillon Charley's peyote religion, and everything seems to lead back to what happened at the oil well."

"Or maybe you're just curious," Mary said. "Anyway, you won't be able to find them. It's been thirty years."

"It won't be so hard," Chee said. "They'll probably all be kinfolks of Dillon Charley. He hired them, so they'll be kinfolks. Cousins, or uncles, or in-laws at least. The Navajos not only invented nepotism. We perfected it."

"But thirty years," Mary said. "They'll be dead. Or half of them will be."

"One or two, probably," Chee said. "We know Dillon Charley is. But the odds are about four of them are still around." They were outside now, walking across the bricked mall south of the library with the brittle sycamore leaves underfoot and the heatless light of the setting sun throwing their shadows a hundred yards ahead and turning the craggy east face of the Sandia Mountains the color of diluted blood. Chee thought of that, and of Hunt walking fifty feet behind them, and of the target they would make for someone standing at any of the walkways or balconies that overlooked the mall.

"And what can they remember about thirty years? Probably not much."

"Who knows?" Chee said. He thought. Probably nothing with any real accuracy. But there was no other lead to follow. And if nothing else, hunting survivors of the People of Darkness would take him out on the reservation. He would take Mary with him. On the reservation, the blond man would never know where to look for them.

22

A DAY LATER, Chee had taken a fruitless shot in the dark and added a few details to his list of names of Dillon Charley's People of Darkness.

The shot in the dark had taken him to the university's Geology Department library. With some help from a cooperative graduate student, he had found a copy of the geologist's log of the oil well. "It looks fairly typical of that area," the student told him. "There's been some shallow production from the Galisteo formation." He checked through it quickly. "Looks like they found the formation but not the oil."

"You see anything unusual about it?" Chee asked. The log was totally incomprehensible to him. He stared at the sheet of symbols and notations, feeling foolish.

"I'm no authority on Valencia County petroleum geology," the young man said. "But it looks like what I'd expect. What are you looking for?"

"That's the trouble," Chee said. "I don't know."

His luck in hunting Charley's roustabout crew had been only a little better. He and Mary had driven to the reservation and spent the remaining hours of daylight jolting over the washboard back roads and wagon trails of the Checkerboard, hunting information to go with the names extracted from the *Grants Beacon*. By nightfall the list had looked like this:

Roscoe Sam, Ojo Encino or Standing Rock. Mud Clan. Dead. Confirmed.

Joseph Sam, Ojo Encino or maybe Pueblo Pintado area. Mud Clan and married into Salt Clan. One report he died in the 1950s. Others say no.

Windy Tsossie. Mud Clan. Married into Standing Rock Clan. Used to live around Heart Butte? May be dead?

Rudolph Becenti. Mud Clan. Coyote Canyon? Married?

Woody Begay. Mud Clan. Sister lives at Borrego Pass?

It had been generally frustrating, except for Roscoe Sam who had got sick at Tuba City and died in the BIA hospital there, and was remembered as being dead. Joseph Sam was another matter. A distant cousin on the paternal side of the family thought, rather vaguely, that he, too, was dead. Another even more distant paternal-side cousin said he'd moved his wife's sheep and his own belongings over to the Cañoncito Reservation and probably still lived there. Dead or alive, no one had seen Joseph Sam for years. It was the same for the rest of them. An in-law remembered that Rudolph Becenti had moved to Los Angeles but had heard he'd come back again. Windy Tsossie was recalled dimly and unfavorably by a few of his contemporaries around Ambrosia Lakes as one of the Tsossie "outfit" which had lived at Coyote Canyon but had moved away a long time ago. Except for Roscoe Sam, definitely and specifically dead and buried, the day had produced nothing concrete. As for Woody Begay, there was only an old woman's memory that his sister lived north of the Borrego Pass chapter house, and his sister's name was Fannie Kinlicheenie.

The vagueness of it had puzzled Chee. It was almost as if these People of Darkness existed only in shadowy rumors and not as flesh and blood. Even the site of the oil well explosion eluded them. The hunt for Roscoe Sam had taken them near the place where Chee's notes said it had been. They found only the immense dusty hole that was the Red Deuce—a dozen gigantic power shovels eating the earth in a pit that was already two hundred yards deep and a half mile across. The oil well site, too, seemed part of a memory of something that never was.

But Fannie Kinlicheenie was definitely flesh and blood. She had looked out the doorway of her house at them when they drove up. Chee parked his patrol car a polite thirty yards from the residence, thereby respecting a modest people's tradition of privacy. When Fannie Kinlicheenie was ready to receive guests she would let them know. Meanwhile they would wait. Chee offered a cigaret to Mary, and she took it.

"I shouldn't smoke these things," she said, as he lit it for her.

"Neither should I," Chee said.

"This guy's going to be dead, too," Mary said. "Either that or moved way off somewhere."

Chee had a feeling she was right. Otherwise, someone would have remembered him.

"You're too pessimistic," Chee said.

"No. I'm a realist. There's four of them left. After thirty years, you'd have a mortality rate of about twenty-five percent. I think Woody Begay's the one."

Chee considered this logic. He exhaled a cloud of cigaret smoke.

"You started with six," he said. "We got Dillon Charley dead, and Roscoe Sam dead. That's already a thirty-three percent mortality."

Mary didn't comment for a moment.

Then she said, "If you think like that you should avoid poker games. What happened in the past doesn't affect the mathematics. It doesn't affect the probabilities. Forget the other two. Now we have the names of four men who were alive thirty years ago. Chances are one of the four is dead now and three of them are alive."

"Okay," Chee said. "I'll buy that. Now tell me how you figure the dead one will be Woody Begay."

"That's intuition," Mary said. "Women have intuition."

Chee reached for the key in the ignition. "Any use sticking around, you think? Wasting Fannie's time."

Mary grinned at him. "As long as we've come this far, maybe we might as well confirm the hunch."

"I'd like to," Chee said. "Sure you won't be insulted?"

"Naw," she said. "I was wrong once."

"But not recently," Chee said.

"I think I was four." She paused. "No, as a matter of fact, make that twice I was wrong. The second time was being dumb enough to go along on this Great Jimmy Chee Manhunt. Boy, am I tired. How far did we drive today?"

"I don't know," Chee said. "Maybe two hundred and fifty miles. It just seems longer because a lot of it was dirt roads."

"It seems like a thousand," Mary said. "This thing rides like a truck. I think you have too much air in the tires."

"We put in the specified amount," Chee said. "It's intended to jar us around enough so we don't doze off while driving."

"Come to think of it, there was another time I was wrong." She glanced at him and looked quickly away. "That was at the auction, when I got the impression you were interested in me."

"I am," Chee said.

"I mean romantically. You're interested in me because I'm an Anglo. Questions all day long. I feel like I'm being interviewed by a sociologist."

"Anthropologist," Chee said. "And that's the

same reason you came along with me. 'What's this Navajo Indian really like?' You just won't admit it."

Mary laughed. "I admit it," she said. "Now I know what you're really like. You're weird."

"But who knows," Chee said. "Maybe something great will grow out of it. We had a Shakespeare teacher at UNM who said that Romeo was doing a paper on the Capulets for his social studies class. He just wanted to pick Juliet's mind."

"I think he was the Capulet," Mary said. "She was a Montague."

" 'What's in a name?' " Chee recited. " 'A rose by any other name . . .' "

"So what's your secret name?" Mary asked.

"Rose," Chee said. "Something like that."

The Kinlicheenie house was of wood-frame construction, insulated with black tar paper. It sat on an expanse of sandstone elevated enough to offer a fine view of a rolling, eroded landscape—gray-silver sage and black creosote brush.

On the horizon Mount Taylor dominated, as it dominated everything in the Checkerboard. Its top was white, but its slopes were blue and serene. Behind the house was a circular stone hogan, its doorway facing properly eastward. And behind that stood a small Montgomery Ward steel storage shed and the humped roof of the dugout where the family took its sweat baths. "Ever notice how Navajos always build their houses where they have a view?" Chee asked.

"I've noticed that Navajos build their houses as

far as they can possibly get from other Navajos," Mary said. "Any significance to that?"

"We don't like Indians," Chee said.

Mrs. Kinlicheenie was at the door now. Her hair was neatly tied in a bun, and she was wearing a heavy silver squash-blossom necklace and a wide silver-and-turquoise bracelet. Mrs. Kinlicheenie was ready to receive guests.

23

"MY BROTHER?" Fannie Kinlicheenie's expression was puzzled. "You want to find him?"

They were in the front room of the house. The chair in which Jim Chee sat was covered with a stiff green plastic. He felt the chill of it through his uniform shirt. The house was the "summer hogan" of the Kinlicheenies. There was no heating stove in it. In a while, when the high country frost arrived full force, the family would shift its belongings into the old earth-and-stone "winter hogan" and abandon this poorly insulated structure to the cold. Until then, the problem of the chilly margin between the seasons was solved by wearing more layers of clothing. Fannie Kinlicheenie looked about eight layers deep. Chee wished he had worn his jacket in from the patrol car.

"We heard this man was your brother," Chee said. "We need some information from him."

"But he's dead," Fannie Kinlicheenie said. "He's been dead for . . ." She paused, trying to put a date on it. "Why, he was dead when I got married, and that was 1953."

Chee glanced at Mary. "I didn't know that," he said.

Fannie Kinlicheenie was frowning at him.

"Why did you want to talk to him?"

"He used to be a member of the peyote church. The one over by Grants. We wanted to ask him about that."

"Those sons-a-bitches," Fannie Kinlicheenie said in English. "What you want to know about them?"

"About something that happened way back. Your brother and some of them were working on an oil well. The peyote chief warned them not to go one day, and the well blew up while they were away."

"I know about that," Fannie said. "I was a girl then and I was in that peyote church, too. I was the water carrier. You know about that?"

"Yes," Chee said. He didn't know everything about the Native American Church, but he knew the water carrier, usually a woman, played a minor role in the ritual.

"Those sons-a-bitches," she repeated. "There was . . ." She paused, glanced at Mary, and back at Chee. They had been speaking in English, the language shared by all three. Now Fannie Kinlicheenie shifted languages. "There was witches in that church," she said in Navajo. One talked cautiously of witches. One discussed them with strangers reluctantly. One talked of them not at all in front of those who were not members of the People. Mary was not Dinetah—not of the People.

"How do you know they were witches?" Chee asked. He stuck to English. "Sometimes people get blamed for being skinwalkers when they're not."

Fannie Kinlicheenie answered in Navajo. "They gave my brother corpse sickness," she said.

"Maybe he ran into a witch somewhere else."

"It was them," she said. "There were other things. There was that oil well that blew up that year. They pretended the Lord Peyote told them it was going to happen. They told everybody that the Lord sent a vision to tell them not to go to work that day. But the witches blew up that oil well. That's how they knew it was going to happen."

"How do you know that?" Chee asked. He had forgotten to speak English. In fact, he had forgotten Mary, who sat there listening and looking puzzled.

"I just know it," Fannie Kinlicheenie said.

Chee considered this. An irrelevant thought intruded. In a white man's home there would not be this complete silence. There would be the ticking of a clock, the sounds refrigerators make, the noise of a TV coming from somewhere. Here there was no sound at all. No traffic noise. No sirens. Outside it was sunset now; even the breeze was still.

"My aunt," Chee said, using a young man's title of respect for an older woman, "I have come a long way to talk with you here because what you know may be very important. I think that something very bad happened at that oil well and that people may still die because of it. If Navajo Wolves did it, then I think we are still dealing with the same bunch of witches. Can you tell me how you knew Navajo

Wolves blew up that oil well? Did somebody tell you?"

"Nobody told me. Just my own head."

"How was that?"

Fannie Kinlicheenie thought about how to answer.

"My brother got sick. He had pains in his middle here." Fannie indicated her stomach. "Where the spirit is. And pains in his legs. We got a hand trembler to come in and find out what was wrong. The hand trembler said a witch had done it to him. He found a little bump on the back of Woody's head where the witch had put the corpse powder in. Then another one of them got sick, and they got the hand trembler for him. And he'd been witched, too. And the hand trembler said to have an Enemy Way for both of them." Fannie Kinlicheenie paused, organizing what she wanted to say.

"What's going on?" Mary asked.

Chee held up his hand. "Just a minute," he said. And then to the Kinlicheenie woman: "Another one got sick, you said. You mean another member of the church?"

"It was Roscoe Sam," Fannie said. "One of the bunch that worked at the oil well with Woody. One of them that called themselves the People of Darkness."

"Ah," Chee said. He was speaking in English again, conscious of Mary's curiosity. "And the hand trembler said to have an Enemy Way? To do that right, you have to know who the witch is. Who . . ."

"That's right," Fannie Kinlicheenie said. "They did the Enemy Way for both of them, and it was done right. Both of them got better for a while, but then they had to take Woody off to the hospital at Gallup and he died."

"They don't much believe in Navajo Wolves at the hospital," Chee said. "What did they think he died of?"

"They said it was cancer," Fannie said. "Leukemia got in his blood."

"Does Joseph Sam still live around here?"

"He died too," Fannie Kinlicheenie said. "I heard it was the same thing. Leukemia."

"I'd say that the Enemy Way didn't work too well," Chee said.

"I think they waited too long. But part of it worked. It turned the evil around and pointed it at the Navajo Wolf." Fannie Kinlicheenie's smile was full of malice. "He died, too."

"Do you know who it was?" Chee knew he'd have to wait for an answer and that he might not get one. The Dinee didn't like to talk of the dead, or of witches. Speaking the name of a dead witch was doubly dangerous.

Fannie Kinlicheenie licked her lips.

"It was the peyote chief," she said.

And thus she avoided pronouncing the name of Dillon Charley.

24

THEY JOLTED DOWN THE DIRT TRACK toward the graded road that would take them to the asphalt pavement and back to Crownpoint. The sun was down now. High overhead a strip of feathery cirrus clouds glowed salmon pink in the afterglow. But all around them the landscape was dark. Mary had been saying almost nothing.

"Are you going to tell me what all that was about?" She asked it without looking at him.

Chee glanced at her profile. "The part where she started talking Navajo?"

"And you started talking Navajo. Yes. That part."

"She said some people in the Native American Church were witches, and they gave Woody Begay and Roscoe Sam corpse poisoning, and they both died. And before they died, they held an Enemy Way for them, and that turned the witching around against the witch. And the witch was Dillon Charley, and that's what killed Dillon."

Mary was looking at him now. "What do you think of all that?"

"And she said the witches made the oil well blow up," Chee added. "And that Joseph Sam is dead, too."

"Did she say why they wanted to do that?"

"No," Chee said.

"Did she know? Did you ask her?"

"No," Chee said. "You have to understand about our witches. They wouldn't need a motive in the normal sense. Do you know about Navajo Wolves?"

"I thought I did," Mary said. "Aren't they like the white man's witches, and witches in general, and our Laguna-Acoma witches?" She laughed. "Hyphenated witches," she said. "Only with the U.S. Bureau of Indian Affairs would you get hyphenated witches."

"The way it works with Navajos, witchcraft is the reversal of the Navajo Way. The way the Holy People taught us, the goal of life was *yo'zho'*. No word for it in English. Sort of a combination of beauty/harmony, being in tune, going with the flow, feeling peaceful, all wrapped up in a single concept. Witchcraft is the reverse of this concept, basically. There's a mythology built up around it, of course. You get to be a witch by violating the basic taboos—killing a relative, incest, so forth. And you get certain powers. You can turn yourself into a dog or a wolf. You can fly. And you have power to make people sick. That's the opposite of the good power the Holy People gave us—to cure people by getting them back into *yo'zho'*. Back into beauty. So, to make a long story short, a witch wouldn't have a motive for blowing up an oil well. It's a bad thing to do, blowing people up. That's all the motive a skinwalker needs."

"And she said Dillon Charley was a witch?"

"That's what she said. The families had an Enemy Way and turned the witching spell around, and Dillon Charley died."

"That proves he was the witch?"

"Well, sort of," Chee said. "They'd have to already have him spotted as the witch. Then someone has to get something that belonged to a witch—hair, pair of socks, a hat, something personal. That represents the scalp in the Enemy Way ceremonial. On the last day of the ceremonial, the scalp is shot with an arrow. If everything has been properly done, and they have the right witch, this causes the witch to get sick and die from his own spell."

"And the patient gets well?"

"That's the way it works. But it didn't work for our friend Woody. And it didn't work for Roscoe Sam."

The patrol car jolted into a shallow wash and out again. The cloud overhead had changed from pink to a deep glowing red. "Two more dead," Mary Landon said. "Or three."

"You predicted Woody," Chee said.

"There were six of them to begin with," she said. "Six People of Darkness. Six men who didn't go to work at the oil well. Now Roscoe Sam is dead, and Joseph Sam and Begay, and Dillon Charley."

"Leaves Windy Tsossie and Rudolph Becenti," Chee said. "And so far nobody knows where to find them."

"That's too many dead," Mary Landon said.

"They wouldn't be all that old. Probably late middle age if they were alive now. But they died a long, long time ago. When they were pretty young. Just a few years after the oil well. That's too many to be dead." She looked at him thoughtfully. "You think somebody poisoned them all? Something like that? Maybe revenge?"

"As far as we know, Begay died of leukemia," Chee said. "Same thing with Roscoe Sam. Dillon Charley died in the hospital. Vines says he told him he had some sort of cancer. Anyway, in a hospital they'd have detected poison if it was that."

"With an autopsy?" Mary asked.

Chee drove a little while. "I think you're thinking the same thing I'm thinking," he said. "You're thinking about Emerson Charley."

"Yes," Mary said. "I'm thinking about how Emerson Charley didn't have an autopsy."

"Because somebody stole his body out of the cold room at BCMC," Chee said.

"Which seems a funny thing to steal."

"Right," Chee said.

"Unless you don't want an autopsy performed."

"Right," Chee said.

"Which is also what you'd get if you blow the guy into little pieces by bombing his truck. No autopsy. Right?"

"Yeah," Chee said.

"Yeah," Mary said. "Yeah, or maybe baloney. Why would anyone want to poison Emerson Charley? Or Dillon Charley? Or Woody Begay, or any of those guys?"

"No reason," Chee said. "But you know what? Let's go to Albuquerque and see what we can find out at the hospital."

"I don't know," Mary Landon said. "When I go places with you, it's no picnic." She hesitated. "Do you think he'll be there?" She didn't have to say the blond man. Chee knew what she meant.

"I've thought about that," Chee said. "If I was him, I wouldn't go near that hospital. And if I was looking for you and me, that would be the last place I'd look."

25

THE DOCTOR'S NAME was Edith Vassa. The midmorning sun slanted through the window behind her desk and flashed through her short reddish hair. She was a young woman with that pink complexion which made Jimmy Chee wonder why the white men called Indians redskins. Dr. Vassa was the physician who had treated Emerson Charley at the University of New Mexico Cancer Research and Treatment Center. Thus she had been stuck with the job of trying to find out what had happened to the Charley corpse. It had been a frustrating, embarrassing dead end. Edith Vassa was sick of it. Her expression showed it.

"I can tell you everything I know in a very few words. Emerson Charley's vital signs ceased at approximately 5:13 P.M. The physician on duty made the usual examination and certified death. The body was tagged for autopsy and moved to the morgue cold room. The next morning, the morgue attendant noticed he had only one body instead of two. He guessed the body had gone to the morphology laboratory without being properly checked out." Dr. Vassa made an impatient gesture with her hands. "To skip the unnecessary details, it was finally learned that the body had disappeared."

"You presume it was stolen?"

"I presume his relatives collected him," Dr. Vassa said. "The Albuquerque police thought we might have just misplaced it somewhere." She laughed, but she didn't think it was funny.

"All we actually know is that one of the morgue carts was found the next morning in the hallway near the loading dock. Presumably it was used to move the body. And we found that the bag of personal effects that belonged to a second body in the morgue was also missing. It seems safe to presume that someone got into the morgue, picked up the wrong bag of personal effects, put the bag on the cart with the body, rolled it down the hallway to the loading dock, and loaded everything into a car or something."

"It was being held for an autopsy?"

"It was supposed to be held for an autopsy."

"Why the autopsy?"

"It's the routine. We're studying cancer. How it affects cells. How treatment affects tumors. Effect of treatment on blood platelets. On bone marrow. Metastasis. So forth."

"Metastasis?"

"Spreading. How cancer spreads from one part of the body to another."

"You didn't suspect foul play?" Chee asked.

Dr. Vassa smiled, very faintly. "You don't get leukemia through foul play. It's not like a poison. And it's not like an infectious disease, which you could cause by inserting a bacteria. It's caused by . . ." Dr. Vassa hesitated.

Jimmy Chee waited, curious. How would this woman describe the origins of leukemia to a Navajo?

"We don't know exactly what causes it. Perhaps some sort of virus. Perhaps some malfunction in the bone marrow, where blood cells are produced."

Fair enough, Chee thought. He couldn't have done better himself.

"And it's rare, especially among adults?"

"Relatively," Dr. Vassa said. "I think the current case rate for all sorts of malignancies this year is less than three per thousand. Leukemic diseases are about one percent of that. Say three in a hundred thousand."

"Three per thousand?" Mary Landon said. "What would you think of a situation in which you had six men, friends, members of the same church, sort of distant relatives, and three of them die of cancer?"

"I'd be surprised," Dr. Vassa said.

"How surprised?" Mary Landon asked. "Three out of six instead of three out of a thousand."

"It would be quite a coincidence," Dr. Vassa said, "but things like that can happen. Mathematical probabilities work in odd ways. Was Emerson one of the three?"

"He was the son of one of the three," Chee said.

"His father died of cancer?"

"That's what we're told," Mary said.

"But you don't know for sure?" Dr. Vassa asked. "Did they all live in the same area? Work at the same jobs? I think if they really did all die of cancer our epidemiology people would be interested." Dr. Vassa smiled. "Especially if it happened to be cancer of the gall bladder. They're fascinated by that." She reached for the phone. "I'll make you an appointment with Sherman Huff."

Sherman Huff's office was in the basement. Dr. Huff asked questions and took notes, and picked up the telephone. "Three out of six is unusual," he said. "So first we try to find out if the tumor registry has them." He spoke into the telephone, identifying himself and reading the names of Dillon Charley, Roscoe Sam, and Woody Begay off his notes. He kept the receiver pinned to his ear with a raised shoulder and turned back to Chee and Mary Landon.

"Just be a minute or two," he said. "It's a matter of checking the names with the computer. The registry tries to keep a file on every cancer case diagnosed in the state, but these were way back when they were first setting it up. And it could be they were out on the reservation, where they weren't diagnosed."

"In other words, if you don't have the names registered, it won't necessarily mean they didn't have cancer?"

"Not from the early 1950s it won't," Huff said. "And not from the Navajo reservation. However, even in those days, they were getting most of them. They had a pretty good . . ."

The telephone said something into Huff's ear. "Just a second," he said.

He made a note. "Okay," he said. He wrote again. "Thanks. Pull the folders for me. I'll want to look at them." He hung up and glanced at Chee.

"Dillon Charley, leukemia. Roscoe Sam, malignancy affecting liver and other vital organs. Woody Begay, leukemia." Huff's face was thoughtful. "That's a hell of a lot of cancer," he said. "And a lot of leukemia for men their ages."

"And Emerson Charley," Mary Landon added. "He also died of leukemia."

"That's what Vassa told me," Huff said. "Let's make sure. Let's get that folder, too." He dialed the phone again.

"While you have them, give them some more names," Chee said. "Give them Rudolph Becenti, Joseph Sam, and Windy Tsossie."

"Those the other three of the six? You hear they had cancer, too?"

"All we know is that Joseph Sam probably died back in the 1950s, and we couldn't find Becenti or Tsossie," Chee said.

"Tumor registry data is confidential," Huff said. "I can confirm a cancer death for law enforcement. I'm not sure I can just go on a fishing expedition for you."

"I'm only trying to confirm that their cause of death was cancer. It saves me time. Otherwise, I'd have to go hunting for death certificates in county courthouses."

Huff talked into the telephone again. He asked for the Emerson Charley file and a check on Tsossie, Becenti, and Joseph Sam. Then he waited, phone to ear. He was a burly man, with a gray mustache merging into a bushy gray beard, sun-weathered skin, and bright blue eyes. Behind him, the wall was covered with posters: "Smoke Can Make Your Doctor Rich." "Little Orphan Annie's Parents Smoked." "Stamp Out Old Age: Smoke!" "To Kill a Mockingbird: Blow Smoke on It." In the silence, Chee became conscious of a tapping. Mary's little finger was drumming against the arm of her chair. The telephone receiver made a sound.

"Go ahead," Huff said. He wrote on his note pad. "Okay," he said. "I'd like to see them all." He hung up and sat for a moment looking silently at what he had written. "Well," he said.

"Another one?" Mary asked.

"Rudolph Becenti," Dr. Huff said. "Another form of leukemia."

"That's four out of six," Mary Landon said.

"That sure is," Dr. Huff said. "That's a hell of a high percentage."

"How about the other two?" Chee asked. "Tsossie and Joseph Sam?"

"Neither name showed up," Huff said. He was frowning. "Four out of six," he said. "What in the world could account for that? What were they doing?"

"In 1948 they were the members of a roustabout crew on an oil well out near Grants," Chee said. "The common labor. Beyond that they were all members of the same little cult in the Native American Church."

"They ever work in the uranium mines out there? We think we had a little increase from that. But that was lung cancer."

"Not as far as we know. And the mining was just getting well started in Ambrosia Lakes when these guys were dying," Chee said.

"How about asbestos? Were they installing insulation?" He shook his head. "No. Inhaled asbestos fiber is a carcinogen, but nothing like this. Nothing like four out of six. And not that quickly. And it's the wrong kind of cancer. You know anything else about them?"

"Damn little," Chee said.

"Did they ever work up at the Nevada test site? Did they work up there when we were doing that atmospheric testing of the bombs?"

"I don't know," Chee said. "It's not likely."

"That could explain it," Huff said. "We just found out this fall that we had a whole rash of leukemia fatalities downwind from the test site in the middle of the 1950s. We've pinned down twelve cases in one tiny little community. Blood cell formation is particularly sensitive to some forms of radiation."

"I know Dillon Charley didn't work anywhere near Nevada," Chee said. "He was working at Mount Taylor until just before he died."

"As for Emerson Charley," Mary said, "they stopped atmospheric testing years ago, and he just died."

Huff looked disappointed. "Yes," he said, "but

sometimes it takes years to develop. And the cases might not all be connected." He produced a wry smile. "And also, of course, maybe none of them have been within a thousand miles of the test site. Do you think you could find the other two of the six?"

"We can keep trying on Tsossie," Chee said. "But Joseph Sam's dead. He won't do you any good."

"Actually, he might do us some good," Huff said. "Some kinds of cancers affect bone tissue. Some other kinds leave their traces in bone when they metastasize. You can often find the damage in ribs, or vertebrae, or sometimes large marrow bones. Do you know where he's buried?"

"We can try to find out," Chee said.

"And we'll try to find some sort of common denominator among them," Huff said. "How about this church they all belong to?"

"Native American Church," Chee said. "The peyote church."

Huff grinned through his beard. "If we suspected peyote of being carcinogenic, we'd have our mystery solved. But it isn't. Anything else? Anything that ties them all together?"

Chee told him of Dillon Charley's peyote vision, which had saved them all from the oil well explosion, and of the survivors being joined, or so it seemed, in their own cult—the People of Darkness.

"With a mole as their amulet figure? Isn't the fetish usually a predator? A mountain lion, or a bear, or something like that?" Huff asked.

"The mole's the predator of darkness," Chee said.

"But it *is* unusual to use him for an amulet."

"So why did they pick the mole?" Huff asked.

"I've wondered," Chee said. And as he said it, he had a thought. "Whoever took Emerson Charley's body left his personal effects. Could we take a look at them?"

"Why not?" Huff said. "If we haven't lost them, too."

26

THE RED PLASTIC BAG was in a storage room on the second floor among scores of identical plastic bags, all arranged in alphabetical order.

"Bracken," the attendant said. "Caldwell. Charley. Here it is. Emerson Charley. You can take a look at it there on that table."

Chee removed a crushed black felt hat, a pair of cowboy boots which needed half soles, a denim jacket, a Timex watch with a steel band, a plaid cotton shirt, a T-shirt, a pair of jockey shorts, a pair of worn denim jeans, socks, a set of car keys, a pocket knife, a small leather pouch attached to a long leather thong, two blue shoestrings, a package of paper matches, and a billfold. He put the leather pouch and the billfold aside and quickly explored all the pockets. They were empty. Then he inspected the billfold. It contained a five, two ones, a driver's license, a social security card, and a card identifying the agent who had written the liability policy on Charley's pickup truck.

Then he picked up the leather pouch.

"What's that?" Mary asked. "What are you looking for?"

"It's where you carry your ceremonial stuff," Chee said. "Supposed to be made of the hide of a deer killed in the ritual fashion. It holds your gall medicine. What you use against witchcraft. A little pollen. Maybe a little ceremonial corn meal. . . ." He pulled open the draw cord and fished into the pouch with his fingers. "And it's where you carry your amulet, if you carry one."

The amulet he extracted was black, and dull, and shaped into the eyeless, sharp-nosed form of a mole. He held it up for Mary's inspection. It was heavy, formed from a soft stone. Some sort of shale, Chee guessed. "Here we have Dine'etse-tle," Chee said. "The predator of the nadir. The hunting spirit of the underworld. One of the People of Darkness."

He stared at it, heavy on his palm, hoping for some information. It was well formed—better than most amulets. Chee remembered the amateur sculpture in B. J. Vines' huge office. Had Vines made this? Was this formed from one of those fragments of black rock Emerson Charley had found in Vines' keepsake box? Perhaps. But what did that mean? He slipped the mole back into the pouch.

"Did it tell you anything?"

Chee recited two lines of Navajo. "That's from one of the blessing chants," he said.

The mole, his hunting place is darkness.
The mole, his hunting song is silence.

27

THE SECRETARY from Dr. Huff's office met them as they left the storage room. The message was from Chee's Crownpoint office. It told him to call Martin at Albuquerque FBI headquarters.

"I thought nobody knew where we are," Mary said. She was frowning. "Wasn't that how we were going to stay safe?"

"Nobody but my office," Chee said.

"But if your office knows, can't somebody else . . . ?"

"How?" Chee asked.

Mary thought about it, still frowning. She shrugged. "I guess you're right," she said. "But you know how people are."

Martin wanted to remind Chee that he was supposed to come in and look at photographs.

"Maybe in a day or two," Chee said. "To tell the truth, I'm going to stay away from places where this guy might be waiting around for me."

"I think you can relax a little now. He's gone."

"How do you know?"

"We made a clean sweep," Martin said. "Checked every motel, every hotel, every place he could be staying. We even checked new apartment rentals."

"Lot of work," Chee said.

"He's no place around here," Martin said. "And we found the green-and-white Plymouth. It was in a little garage in Gallup. The son of a bitch drove it in and told the mechanic it needed a valve job and he was in no hurry for it. That's why we didn't find it abandoned anywhere."

"That was smart," Chee said. "You know how he got out of Albuquerque this time?"

"We're pretty sure he stole a car. Just drove it somewhere. Maybe El Paso or Denver. Somewhere far enough to miss our stakeouts. And then he took a plane for wherever he goes."

"So he's not in Albuquerque?"

"Not unless he's staying with relatives," Martin said.

28

AT THE COST OF HOURS of driving from here to there in search of older members of the Mud Clan, Jimmy Chee learned a little about Windy Tsossie. He learned that not long after the oil well explosion, Tsossie had married a daughter of Grace Yazzie of the Standing Rock Clan. He had moved northwestward to the Bisti country to join his new family. He had been seen around Ambrosia Lakes no more. Chee learned that Tsossie's wife was dead. He learned other things as well. Among the important ones was that Tsossie's sister-in-law, a woman named Romana Musket, was alive and well and living between Thoreau and Crownpoint in the log house with the tin roof and the sheep pens behind it that was visible on the slope above the highway. Mrs. Musket seemed likely to know where Tsossie could be found, alive or dead. Chee had also learned that no one seemed to know for sure which one it would be. No one had heard Tsossie had died. On the other hand, Chee had found no one who had actually seen him for years. And finally Chee had accumulated a general impression of Windy Tsossie. It was a negative impression. His kinsmen and his clansmen, when they admitted remembering him at all, remembered him without fondness or respect. They talked of him reluctantly, vaguely, uneasily. No one put it in words. Since Chee was Navajo, no one needed to. Windy Tsossie did not "go in beauty." Windy Tsossie was not a good man. He did not follow those rules which Changing Woman had given the People. In a word, Windy Tsossie was believed by his kinsmen to be a witch.

"I don't see how you can say that," Mary said. "You told me what they said. Nobody even hinted at anything like that."

"They wouldn't," Chee said, "not to a stranger. I might be a witch myself. Or you might be. And witches don't like people talking about witches."

Mary yawned. "You're stretching things," she said.

"Did you notice that talking about Tsossie made them nervous? That's the tip-off."

"The thing that interests me is I think we're finally going to find one of them alive," she said. "What's he going to tell us? I really think now he's going to remember something."

"If he's alive."

"He will be."

"I have the same sort of hunch," Chee said.

They were driving the subagency's pickup truck, having traded the relative comfort of the patrol car for the ability to follow wagon tracks. They drove northeastward, mostly in second gear, over a rutted road which now tilted downward. Chee flicked his lights to bright. The beams lit the broad, sandy bottom of an arroyo below. When they reached it, he stopped.

"Chaco Wash," he said. He switched on the dome light, unfolded his map, and examined it. The map was one entitled "Indian Country," produced by the Auto Club of Southern California; Chee had found it both accurate and detailed. It rated routes of travel in nine categories, ranging from Divided Limited Access Highways, down through Gravel, Graded Dirt, and Ungraded Dirt to Doubtful Dirt. For the last fifteen miles, they had been driving on Doubtful Dirt. According to the map, the Doubtful Dirt ended at Chaco Wash.

Chee folded the Indian Country map and extracted from his shirt pocket a lined sheet of notebook paper. It had come from a red-covered Big Chief notebook at the home of Mrs. Musket. On it, a grandson of Ramona Musket had drawn another map to show how to reach the hogan where Rudolph Charley was conducting a Peyote Way. His grandmother was attending the services. The grandson was about twelve. He wore a T-shirt with the S symbol of Superman decorating its front, and he drew the map carefully with a ballpoint pen, and while he drew he explained that Rudolph Charley was the new peyote chief because somebody had shot the old peyote chief, who was Rudolph Charley's older brother.

"Right at Chaco Wash the regular road got washed out," Supergrandson said. "You turn right there, and you drive up the sand if you want to, because it's smoother. You got to pay attention or you'll miss the turns. I'll put down some landmarks to look for." He glanced up and grinned at Mary, and switched politely to English. "If you're not careful out there you can get lost," he assured her.

On the Big Chief map, Supergrandson had penned in "salt cedars" at the point where the Doubtful Dirt road petered out at the wash bottom. Now, in the beam of his headlights, Chee could see a cluster of winter-bare salt cedar below. Chee let the truck roll forward again, past the trees and onto the smoothness of the arroyo floor.

"Here's where we get to the place where if we're not careful we can get lost," Mary said. "Is that right?"

"Right," Chee said.

"Let's not," Mary said. "I'm too tired. I'm flat out exhausted. It seems like we've been in this truck about seventeen days."

"Just since about sunrise," Chee said.

Mary turned suddenly and stared back out the rear window. "I get a feeling I'll look back there and see somebody following us," she said. "Not somebody. That blond man."

"How could he?" Chee asked. "There's no way he could know where we're going."

She shivered, and hugged herself. "Let's say he's smart," she said. "Or let's say he has some reason himself to go to this peyote ceremony."

"I can't think why he would."

"It's a memorial service for Tomas Charley, isn't it? Or something like that. Maybe he's looking for people, just as we are. Maybe we'll just run into him there."

"I doubt it," Chee said.

"I think you're like me. Too tired to care. You're so tired you're going to tell me your war name."

"It won't be much longer now," Chee said. "We want to be at Charley's place at midnight, and then Mrs. Musket will tell us that Windy is living in Grants and give us his address and telephone number. Then we go get some sleep and tomorrow we'll call Tsossie, and he'll tell us who blew up the oil well and why, and where to find the evidence to give to the grand jury, and who to arrest and why Emerson Charley's body was taken out of the hospital, and who hired the blond man to shoot Tomas Charley, and . . ."

"Oh, stop," Mary said. She yawned hugely behind her hand. "With the luck you and I have," she said through the end of the yawn, "that kid gave us the wrong address or the wrong night, or Mrs. Musket won't be there, or she never heard of Windy Tsossie, or she won't like your looks and won't talk to you, or she'll tell you Tsossie moved to Tanzania and didn't leave an address, or it's the wrong Tsossie, or the blond will be there and he'll shoot you. Or even worse, he'll shoot me."

Chee smiled. "Well," he said, "we'll soon know."

At seven minutes to midnight the track they were following skirted a rocky outcrop covered with stunted juniper. The truck's headlights reflected from a windshield, and then from the corrugated metal roof of a shack and the glass of the window below the roof. Chee slowed the truck to a crawl and examined what the headlights showed him. Three pickup trucks, an old white Chevy, and a wagon on which bales of hay served as seats. Twenty yards behind the shack was the round stone shape of a hogan, with a thin wisp of blue smoke emerging from the smoke hole in the center of its conical dirt-insulated roof. No one was in sight.

Chee parked the truck beside the newest of the pickups, flicked off the headlights, and stepped out into the darkness. The moon was down and the black sky was brilliant with a billion stars. He stood with face raised, drinking it in—the great fluorescent sweep of the Milky Way, the pattern of the winter constellations, the incredible silent brightness of the universe.

Mary was standing beside him now. "My God," she said in a hushed voice. "I never saw the sky like that."

"Altitude," Chee said. "We're almost at the Continental Divide here. Mile and a half above sea level; air's thin. And partly it's because there's no ground lights. Look," he said, pointing to the southeast. "See that little glow on the horizon? That's Albuquerque. Hundred miles away, but you can see what it does."

"It makes you forget for a minute how cold you

are," Mary said. She shuddered. "The minute's up. I'm cold."

From the hogan came the sound of song and the tapping of a pot drum. Distance and the hogan walls muted it, and the singing was not much more than a rising and falling rhythm, part of the background of the windless night. Chee glanced at his watch. The followers of Lord Peyote wouldn't recess their ceremonial until midnight. They began at sunset after a prayer to inform the setting sun that their intentions were holy, and the ritual would not end until sunrise. But at midnight there was a break. And that meant another five minutes to wait.

"When I was a boy," Chee said, "sometimes my mother would wake me up in the darkest part of the night, and we'd go out away from the hogan, and she'd teach me star lore. How the constellations move and how you can tell the direction and the time of night if you know the time of year. And how it all began."

"How did it all begin?" Mary asked.

"There weren't any Navajos yet. Just Holy People. First Man, First Woman, Talking God, Gila Monster, Corn Beetle, all the various *yei* figures. At night, the sky was black and blank except for the moon. So First Man decided to hang out the stars. And he put up the Blue Flint Boys"—Chee pointed to Cepheus—"and the Bear, and the Stalking God, and all the rest. And along came Coyote, and he grabbed the blanket where First Man had the stars waiting to be hung, and he gave it a toss and threw all that were left out in one great swinging motion. That's what made the Milky Way."

"Quite a coyote," Mary said. She shivered again and hugged herself.

The hogan was silent now, and suddenly there was light at the doorway as the blankets hung across the opening were pulled back.

Chee reached into the cab of the truck and turned on the dome light. It was polite to let people know who was calling on them.

Contrary to Mary's pessimism, Mrs. Musket was there. She was a gray-haired, sturdy woman with a red-and-green mackinaw over the voluminous velveteen blouse and skirt of traditional Navajo womanhood. She wasn't sure she wanted to talk about Windy Tsossie.

Rudolph Charley invited them into the hogan out of the cold, and stood beside them listening. Rudolph Charley looked a lot like Tomas Charley. Just a little younger and even thinner.

"It all happened a long time ago," Chee was saying. "Before he married your sister. There was an explosion at an oil well where he worked. We want to see if he remembers what happened."

Mrs. Musket stared at Chee, glanced nervously at Mary, at Charley, and then back at Chee.

"He won't remember anything," Mrs. Musket said.

"It seems like just about everybody else who was working with Tsossie is dead," Chee said. "We can't talk to them. We want to talk to him."

"I think Windy is dead, too," Rudolph Charley said. "I think the witch got them all."

"Yes," Mrs. Musket said. "He's dead."

"When did he die?" Chee asked. He suspected Mrs. Musket was lying. Experience taught one to watch the face of a person being questioned. Lying made almost everyone nervous. Mrs. Musket was nervous. But then she would be nervous anyway, at being questioned by strangers who appeared out of the darkness to talk of death. And there was more to it than nervousness. Something vague and hard to define. And he thought that he knew what was causing it. Mrs. Musket had eaten peyote and drunk of the "black drink" of the ceremonial—peyote tea. She was in that dreamy world of the psychedelic. He glanced at Rudolph Charley. The road chief of his ceremonial, too, looked at Chee as if he wasn't sure that Chee existed.

"When did he die, then?" Chee repeated. "And where did they put the body?"

"Long time ago," Mrs. Musket said. She stood looking at Chee and through Chee. The seconds ticked away. "They lived out behind Bisti in the badlands. I wasn't with them. But my sister's husband was a witch, and somebody turned the witching around against him. He got corpse sickness and he died."

"You weren't there, but you heard about it? Is that right? From your sister?" Chee asked.

"From my sister," Mrs. Musket agreed.

"He died of a sickness?"

"Corpse sickness," Mrs. Musket said.

"Where?"

"In my sister's hogan."

"And they buried him there?"

"They got a white man who worked there at Bisti to come and put the body out in the rocks. They told me that he put it in a little blowhole in the side of a cliff and covered it over with rocks."

"It's all starting up again," Rudolph Charley said suddenly. "More witching."

Chee looked at him. Charley's eyes were focused somewhere a long way off.

"The first time it killed my grandfather, and all the people who the Lord Peyote let see through the doorway. The witching killed all six of them. And now it has started up again. First it killed my grandfather. Now it has killed my father, and it killed my brother. Tonight we are asking the Lord Peyote to let us see what will happen next. . . ." His voice trailed off.

Mary began a word and bit it off. The four of them stood there, silently, waiting for the road chief to continue. Beyond Charley, Chee could see the room. The packed earthen floor had been cleared of furnishings. The peyote altar had been built across the back of it—a low crescent shape of hard-packed sand. The peyote moon, they called it. At its center, where the sand was perhaps six inches high, a cup-sized bed of cedar twigs had been built. In this nest the gnarled, hairy shape of a peyote button rested. On the sand beside it was a small silver box, lid open.

Behind the peyote moon two zigzag lines were inscribed in the earth, representing the footprints of Christ. The Native American Church as it came to the Checkerboard was more or less Christian. Christ taught the white man only through the Bible, because the white man had crucified him. But the Navajo, who had not harmed Christ, God instructed directly through visions. And Lord Peyote was the instrument, the key to the door which led to reality.

Rudolph Charley still stood motionless, caught in some odd drug-induced expansion of time.

"Did he let you see?" Chee asked.

"I saw the mole," Rudolph Charley said. "The amulet that was my father's and my grandfather's."

"Nothing else?" Chee asked.

The door opened and two men ducked through— both young. They glanced at Chee and at Mary. One added sticks to the piñon fire which had burned to a bed of coals in the hogan fire pit. The other went to the back wall and squatted by the pot drum, watching and waiting. Rudolph Charley's mood changed.

"Nothing you would understand," he said. "We have to start again now. We have to finish the service."

"The man you want to talk to is dead," Mrs. Musket said.

"All right," Chee said. "Then tell me where to find the blowhole where they put his body."

29

FINALLY COLTON WOLF was ready. He'd had both a CB radio and a radiotelephone installed in the cab of the pickup. He had driven up an arroyo east of the Sandia Mountains and refreshed his marksmanship with both his rifle and his .22 caliber pistol. The rifle was an expensive .30 caliber Ruger equipped with a scope. He'd fired off half the shells from a 100-round carton, adjusting the open sights for ranges up to 250 yards and the scope up to 800. Then he'd established with a telephone call to the hospital that Western Union couldn't deliver a telegram to Jim Chee because Jim Chee had checked out. That confirmed what Colton had expected. Next he called the city desk at the *Albuquerque Journal,* identified himself as a professor at the university, and got permission to do some research in the newspaper's library. An hour of reading through clippings of crime reports provided him with the names of FBI agents and sheriff's officers who worked on or around the Navajo reservation. He jotted the names and pertinent information into his notebook and then asked if there was a file on B. J. Vines. There was. The oldest clipping reported a transfer of uranium leases from Vines to a consortium of mining companies headed by Kennecott Copper and Kerr-mac Nuclear Fuels. Another, a wire service story originating in New York, reported that Vines had won the Weatherby Trophy, the world championship of big-game hunting. The only substantial story was a feature, with photographs, of the construction of Vines' home on the slope of Mount Taylor. The residence was described as "probably the most expensive ever built in New Mexico." The man whose name Colton had found in the box he'd been hired to recover was obviously rich enough to pay the cost of recovering it. There was a good chance, then, that Vines was the client. Not a certainty, because someone else seemed to have wanted the box. But Vines seemed most likely. Colton added to his notes a description of the house and its location. If all else failed, that might be useful.

Colton's last stop was at the municipal library, where he checked through the file of telephone books and noted the numbers he might need. And then he drove westward from Albuquerque, climbing out of the Rio Grande valley, crossing the Rio Puerco breaks, and rolling at a steady fifty-five miles an hour across the empty mesa-butte landscape of west central New Mexico. As he drove, he tested his radio reception on the federal and law-enforcement channels. Reception was excellent. The technique and terminology of the radio dispatchers was no different from what he'd heard in other states. Then he tested the telephone connection by calling the U.S. Weather Service for the forecast. For the west central plateau of New Mexico, the forecast was for increasing afternoon cloudiness, periodic gusty winds, and colder temperatures through the afternoon, with a 60 percent chance of snow before midnight. The green interstate information sign told Colton that the Grants interchange was ahead. To his right, Mount Taylor rose against an unnaturally blue sky, its highest slopes white with snowbanks. He let the camper roll to a stop on the shoulder of the highway, picked up the phone, checked his notebook for the names he wanted, and placed a call to the Navajo Tribal Police subagency office at Crownpoint.

The voice that answered was a woman's.

"This is the Federal Bureau of Investigation," Colton said, "Albuquerque. Agent Martin. Is Captain Largo there?"

"He works out of Tuba City," the voice said. "That number . . ."

"I know that," Colton said, "but Largo told me he might stop in there today. How about Jim Chee, then?"

"Chee's not here, either," the voice said. "He's taking some time off."

"How's he feeling? Hope those ribs are healing up."

"Okay, I guess."

"I was calling about Chee," Colton said. "We got

some things we want him to look at. About that shooting. How can I get hold of him?"

"Just a minute," the voice said. There was a pause.

Colton waited. This was the crucial moment. He would allow the delay to stretch four minutes. More than that would risk a successful trace. He couldn't chance the police learning that this was a radiotelephone call. The second hand on his watch dial swept into the second minute.

"We'll have to get him on the radio." It was a man's voice now. "What's the message?"

"Tell him Martin has some information for him, and I need to show him some pictures. Tell him I'm coming out to the reservation and have him call me on my car telephone." He provided a wrong number that sounded reasonable. "Is he near a telephone?"

"I doubt it," the voice said.

"Look," Colton said. "This is urgent. See if you can find him, and if he's a long ways from a telephone, can I get you to call me back and let me know how long it will be?"

"Sure," the voice said.

"Okay. Thanks," Colton said. He hung up, switched on the radio receiver, and pulled the truck back onto Interstate 25. He hadn't gone a mile before he monitored the first call from the Crownpoint dispatcher trying to reach Jimmy Chee.

Colton drove steadily westward, past Grants, past the uranium-processing mills of Ambrosia Lakes, into the rougher country which climbed toward the Continental Divide. Crownpoint was trying to reach

Chee at ten-minute intervals. At the Thoreau interchange, Colton pulled off the highway and parked. It was here he had decided to wait. He had never thought there was a serious chance that Chee would run far after the fiasco in the hospital. There was no need to run. Where better to hide an Indian than on an Indian reservation?

He sat with his knees propped against the dash and put together a sandwich of the materials he had brought from the trailer. As always, he ate slowly. The mountain was miles to the east now, but it still dominated the landscape, cold and ominous. When this was over, when he had caught Jim Chee and killed him, and killed the woman; when his tracks were erased and he was once again secure, then he would find a better way to trace his mother. Perhaps a hypnotist could help him remember something he had forgotten. Something useful. There was that old woman in one of his earliest memories. She had put him on her lap and her breath had smelled of tobacco. He had always guessed she might be a grandmother. If he could remember that—or even the place where they had lived when he was very small—it might be helpful. He could remember so little of that. Only a sense of days of cold fog, days of rain, days in an upstairs apartment with his meals left in a refrigerator, his mother coming home in the mornings, his mother's hair damp against his face, his mother's hands cold against his skin. There were men then, too, but no particular man he could remember.

He was staring outward at the blank blue sky, but

his thoughts were on that room. He could remember the cracks in the gray linoleum. He'd had two marbles then and the marbles would chase one another down the cracks. He could remember playing that game endlessly, day after day, and the grimy windows, but not the name of the town. Surely he had heard it. Surely, even at four or five, it had meant something to him. His mother had not talked to him often. She wouldn't have been likely to tell a child they were living in Seattle, or Portland, or wherever it was. But he must have heard it. He would find himself a hypnotist and maybe then he could remember something. Colton was aware that things were wrong with his memory. Gaps in it. He ran his thumb down his sweater, feeling the bump under the skin where the rib had healed crookedly. He could remember when he didn't have the bump—when they lived in San Diego. He could remember having it, already healed, in Bakersfield. But he couldn't remember the beating that produced it. It was the same with the ridge of thick white scar tissue under the hair above his left ear. That also had grown from some blank spot in his childhood. The last time he had tried to remember about that was in Taylorville, but trying had made him sick and he had stopped.

His radio spoke again, the voice of the Crownpoint dispatcher called for Jim Chee.

This time, Chee answered. Colton put down his sandwich and picked up his notebook. Crownpoint relayed the message he had left.

"Well, hell," Chee's voice said. "We're way over

here by the old Bisti trading post."

Colton jotted "We're by Bisti" on his pad. He underlined "We're."

"If you're away from the telephone, he wanted me to call him and let him know where he could meet you. He said he'd be coming to the reservation," the dispatcher said.

There was a pause. "Well," the voice of Chee said. "I guess he's going to have to wait, then. We're trying to find a hogan northwest of the old trading post. It's about nine miles back in there, and it'll take me a while to find it. Tell him I'll meet him at our office in Crownpoint tonight. Tell him I'll try to be there by nine, but I might be a little late."

"Ten-four," the dispatcher said. "You paying attention to the weather? It's supposed to snow."

"Right," Chee said. "We'll watch it."

Colton jotted "We" on his note pad. He also wrote "nine miles back in there." He didn't make a note of the nine o'clock meeting time at Crownpoint. By nine o'clock Jimmy Chee would be dead.

30

THE BISTI TRADING POST had burned years ago, with the thoroughness with which buildings burn when there is no fire department to interfere. The fire had left only the blackened stone foundation and odds and ends of melted glass and twisted metal. Years of casual Navajo scavengers had sorted through the ashes, and years of weather had piled tumbleweeds and dust against the ruins. The great cypresses imported to protect the post from the sun had long since starved for water, like town dogs abandoned in the desert. The row of bare dead trunks now served as an incongruous landmark for a ruin that had otherwise almost returned to nature.

Chee turned the pickup truck left beyond the dead trees, leaving a road marked "Graded Dirt" for a track his map did not show. It ran, fairly straight and fairly smooth, across an expanse of creosote brush.

"You sure this is the right way?" Mary asked.

"No," Chee said, "but I'm sure it's the right direction."

"And you still think we can find the hogan? After all these years?"

"Probably," Chee said. "She said nine miles northwest by north of the trading post, at the south side of an isolated butte. And she described the butte." He pointed ahead. "That must be it. And out here they'd have had to build the hogan of stone, so it's still there. It's just a matter of hunting it. And I'm pretty good at hunting." Chee paused, thinking about that statement. "Or I used to think I was."

The land sloped downward now, into an immensity of erosion. What once had been a sandstone plain had been carved into a grotesquerie of shapes—tables, heads, layer cakes, twisted spires, exposed ribs, serrations, and weird forms that suggested things to which Chee's imagination could not attach names. Wind and water had cut through the overlay into the blackness of coal deposits, into crimson clay, into the streaky blue of shale. Every color showed except green. This was the Bisti badlands. It stretched away for fifty miles under a sky in which clouds had been steadily building.

"I have a hunch he's not dead," Mary said. "I sort of sensed she was hiding something."

"She was nervous," Chee said. "Maybe she was lying and maybe there was another reason. But if the bones are there, we'll find them. And if they're not, we'll find Tsossie."

As he said it, his confidence surprised him. But he *was* confident. Finding Tsossie, skeletal or breathing, involved things purely Navajo—a pattern of thinking and behavior with which Chee was in intimate harmony. He felt no such harmony with the thinking of the whites who must be involved in this affair. For all enterprises, such harmony was essential. Especially for the hunter. And this was from the very start a hunt.

One of the prayers from the Stalking Way ran through his mind, and the voice of his uncle chanting:

I am the Black God as I sing this,
Black God I am. I come and I stand
beneath the East, beneath the Turquoise
   Mountain.
The crystal doe walks toward me,
as I call it, as I pray to it,
toward me it comes walking, understanding me
it walks this day into my right hand.
Pleasant, it comes to join me,
in its death it obeys the voice of my singing.
In its beauty I obey the crystal doe.

Perfect understanding, Chee thought. Harmony between deer and man. Harmony between Jim Chee and Tsossie, or the bones of Tsossie, and the thinking of those who had placed Tsossie's corpse among the rocks. But Jim Chee didn't understand the thinking of whites. Neither Changing Woman nor Talking God had given him a song to produce that understanding. What would his uncle say to that? Chee knew exactly what the old man would say. He could almost hear him, because he had heard him so often:

"Boy, when you understand the big, you understand the little. First understand the big."

And that would mean, in this case, that if Chee learned to understand all men (the big), he could understand white men (the little). His uncle would add that if a Navajo could find harmony with a deer, he could find equal harmony with a white man. Chee grimaced at the windshield. And then his uncle, who never failed to belabor a point, would add some wisdom about deer and men. He would say that the deer is much like the Navajo in fundamental ways. It loves its offspring and its mate, food, water, and its rest. And it hates cold, hunger, pain, and death. But the deer is also different. Its life is short. It builds no hogans. The Navajo is more like a white man than like a deer.

That's about what his uncle would say, Chee thought sourly. But his uncle had no dealings with the whites when he could avoid them. And how would his uncle explain the thinking of a white man who filled his home with mementos of his achievements but kept his greatest honors hidden away in a keepsake box? The medals Tomas Charley had described were a Bronze Star and a Silver Star, which—as the military encyclopedia in the university library had informed him—are awarded for deeds of courage in combat; and the Purple Heart, awarded to those wounded in action. You would expect to find them framed in places of prominence on Vines' wall, along with his other trophies. Why did he hide them away with a package of old boyhood photographs and a double handful of rock fragments? A Navajo might either advertise his exploits or modestly conceal them. Why would anyone hide some and advertise others?

The sky was darker now and the wind blew from the northwest. It gusted around the pickup, kicking up a flurry of sand and tumbleweeds.

"That has to be our butte," Chee said. He pointed through the right side of the windshield. "It's the only one within nine miles of the trading post. And it's in the right direction."

The track emerged on a great sheet of barren granite and skirted an island of overlaid sandstone. The island was capped by a slab of white limestone, which left a wide overhang where the softer rock had worn away. It suggested to Chee a table where giants dined. Suddenly, just beyond this landmark, he took his foot from the gas pedal and let the truck roll to a stop.

"What?" Mary asked.

Chee looked at her. "Boy," he said. "Am I stupid." He slammed his fist against the steering wheel. Two sets of keepsakes, he was thinking. One on the walls. One hidden in the safe. What was the difference between them? The difference was in time.

Mary was staring at him. "Come on," she said. "Cut it out. Let me in on it."

"I'm still getting it sorted out," Chee said. "But what it boils down to is why a man who's very much into keeping mementos and showing them off would hide the best of them in his wall safe."

"Like those medals," Mary said.

"Like those and his high school football team picture, and a couple of athletic awards."

"And black rocks," Mary said.

"Let's get to those later. Stick to the easy stuff now."

"Easy if you've thought of the answer," Mary said. "Quit showing off, damn it. What have you thought of?"

"The only difference I can see is the ones in the safe were all from Vines' early life. Boyhood and young man in the military. The stuff on the wall is after he struck it rich."

Mary had her lower lip caught between her teeth. Her expression said she was looking for significance in this. "Before the oil well explosion and after the explosion. Is that it? And how about the rocks?"

"We better get moving," Chee said. "It's going to get dark." He put the pickup in gear.

"In other words, you don't know about the rocks."

"Somehow they had to be important. A memento of something important," Chee said. "And from his early life."

"I'll buy that," Mary said. Moments ticked away as the pickup jolted over the rocky surface. "Hey," Mary said. "I know what. The rocks are from when he found the uranium deposit. They're his first ore samples. Don't you think?"

"That would fit," Chee said. "Sure. Why didn't you think of that earlier?"

"You didn't ask me," Mary said. "All you had to do was ask."

"Okay, then. Explain why he keeps those medals in the safe."

"Maybe he's keeping them for somebody else," Mary said.

The wind rocked the pickup again, buffeting it with a barrage of driven sand. Chee down-shifted to pull the truck up a steep incline.

"Mary," he said, "you're a genius." He switched on the transmitter and raised the dispatcher at Crownpoint. His instructions were specific. Call Martin at the FBI. Tell him to have the Veterans Administration make a high-priority emergency check on the military record of Benjamin J. Vines. Was he a first lieutenant in the 101st Airborne Division? Had he won the Silver Star, Bronze Star, and Purple Heart? What kind of discharge? Any criminal record in the service?

The dispatcher read the instructions back. "Anything else?"

"Tell Martin I'll explain it to him when I see him tonight. Tell him I'll be late. And . . . wait a minute." Chee fished out his notebook. "Give him these names, too." He read off the names of those killed in the oil well explosion. At the name of Carl Lebeck, he paused. Lebeck the geologist. Lebeck the well-logger. For a geologist, black rocks might be a memento. "Put the name of Lebeck first," Chee said. "Tell Martin that if Vines didn't win those decorations, to have the VA go down that list of names and see if Lebeck or any of the others won them."

"Got it," the dispatcher said. "You still at Bisti?"

"Northwest of the burned-out trading post," Chee said. "We'll be out here until after dark, the way it looks."

"Better watch the weather," the dispatcher said. "It's snowing some over on the west side. Inch on the ground at Ganado. Not supposed to amount to much, but you know how that is."

"We'll watch it," Chee said. He flicked the radio switch and put the pickup back into gear.

"What are you thinking?" Mary asked.

Chee frowned at the windshield. "Mostly, I'm just taking a shot in the dark."

"But just mostly," Mary said. "Have you figured a way that Vines and the oil well connect?"

"They must," Chee said. "They have to connect. If not Vines, then Gordo Sena. One or the other has to connect."

Mary laughed. "Sure," she said. "Now all you have to do is figure out how."

"I think I have," Chee said. "At least part of it."

The track angled to the right and up the slope of dark-blue shale marbled with reddish impurities. Above it, the top of the butte loomed, now no more than a thousand yards away. Chee shifted down. Mary was watching him impatiently.

"I'm waiting," she said.

"Okay," Chee said. "First we agree there has to be a reason. White man or Navajo, you do things for a reason. With a Navajo, something this bad—blowing up people wholesale—would have to be witch business. Irrational. Evil for the sake of evil. No other motive would make sense. For the white man, I think it would be greed." He glanced at her. "All right so far?"

Mary looked puzzled. "I guess so," she said.

"If we're dealing with witchcraft, what's happened since doesn't connect. Maybe a Navajo would want to kill the Charleys if he knew they were witches who'd done him harm. That's happened. But he would do it in the heat of rage, not years later. So let's set that aside."

Mary shrugged.

"So we're dealing with a white man's crime," Chee continued. "The motive's greed. Who gains by blowing up an oil well? You have to remember where that well was. We couldn't find the remains because the Red Deuce has swallowed up the site. So the oil company drilling the well had a mineral rights lease on that piece of land. If the well produces oil, the lease is extended as long as production lasts. That's the standard oil lease form. So let's say somebody knows there's a uranium deposit under the well. Who'd benefit?"

"You mean the Senas? Because it was on their ranch?"

"Maybe the Senas," Chee said. "When it finally did happen, uranium made Gordo Sena rich. But something doesn't fit with thinking Gordo did it."

"You mean like killing his own brother?" Mary asked. "Maybe Robert Sena planned it himself and then something went wrong and he killed himself, too."

"I didn't mean that," Chee said. "I meant the Sena ranch is like most ranches out here. It's a little bit of privately owned land connected to a big spread of federal Bureau of Land Management land. Most of what you own is a permit to graze your cattle on BLM land. That's where the well was drilling. On federal land. The Senas had the grazing lease, but it was about a quarter of a mile from the boundary of their own land. So they wouldn't benefit directly from either an oil strike or a uranium find. Sena got rich because the uranium deposit spread over onto his family property."

"So you rule out Sena," Mary said. "Who then?"

"I don't quite rule out the Senas," Chee said. "There's a piece missing somewhere. I can't think it through."

The pickup tilted abruptly downward into a narrow wash. Chee shifted into his lowest gear, braked to a stop, and inspected the arroyo. The problem would be pulling the truck up the other side. The arroyo carried very little water even after downpours, and a tall growth of mesquite and rabbit brush on both sides of the track had limited erosion. But still, years of cutting away had made the opposite bank steep enough so that getting traction to the pickup out of it looked chancy.

"Looks like the end of the line," Mary said. "But aren't we close enough to walk?"

"We'll try the pickup," Chee said. "If we don't make it, there's plenty of room down there to turn it around."

The vehicle produced a great shower of flying gravel, lost traction briefly, and skidded sideways. But it made the brief, steep climb. Ahead now, no more than four hundred yards away, they could see three gnarled cottonwoods. In a desert climate they signaled either a spring or a very shallow water sand that could be tapped by a well. And that in turn explained why this track led across the badlands and why the Tsossies had picked the site for their hogan. Chee and Mary could see the hogan now about twenty feet beyond the trees. It was a hexagon of stacked sandstone slabs, roofed with poles which radiated outward from a central smoke hole. The earth that once insulated the roof against cold and heat had long since washed away.

Chee pulled the pickup to a stop against an outcrop of cliff. He clipped on his holster and hung his binocular case around his neck. "Be prepared," he said, and stepped out into the wind.

The doorway of the hogan was closed with planks nailed across the lintel logs. The only opening now was on the north side—a hole knocked through the stone wall to provide an exit for the ghost and to warn strangers that this was a death hogan. Chee stood looking into the hole. The evening light that filtered through the latticework of roof showed nothing but odds and ends of junk too worthless to carry away even by an impoverished family. Dirt had blown in and tumbleweeds had bounced through the ghost hole, but the danger posed by the *chindi* had made the place secure from scavengers.

"If Tsossie didn't die here, someone did," Chee said. "Let's find the place the old lady said they put him."

Mary was staring at the hogan. "I've heard about this," she said, "about Navajos not using buildings after somebody dies in them. It seems awfully wasteful."

"Unless maybe they died of something contagious," Chee said. "When the custom started, I guess that was the purpose."

"They carry the body out the hole? Is that right? Always on the north side?"

Chee didn't want to talk about it now. The wind gusted again, carrying around a light load of dry, feathery snowflakes. "North is the direction of evil," he said.

Mrs. Musket had told them the blowhole was in the mesa wall, west of the hogan. The butte was formed of layers of geological formations, capped with a gray erosion-resistant granite. Below that was a stratum of red sandstone perhaps thirty feet deep, which covered porous, whitish volcanic tuft that had been riddled with wind pockets and seepage holes. Only two of these near the hogan were large enough for a burial. Chee examined both through the binoculars and saw nothing conclusive. They climbed the talus slope toward the nearest one. Against the perpendicular walls of the butte, sections of the soft perlite had been worn away, undermining the sandstone. A section of it had fallen in a clutter of blocks, each as large as a freight car. Chee scrambled up the sloping side of one of the blocks and looked into the blowhole. Rocks had been piled on its floor. From beneath one of them a ragged fragment of blue cloth protruded. The wind eddied into the hole. The cloth fluttered.

"Come on up," Chee said. "I guess we found Windy Tsossie."

Sometimes the dry cold of a desert winter will protect a corpse from decay and turn it into a desiccated mummy. Since the placement in the cliff and the covering of rocks had protected Tsossie from both animal predators and scavenger birds, this might have happened to him. But Tsossie, apparently, had died in the summer, and thirty years of insects had reduced what he had been to a clean white skeleton.

With the last rocks removed, Chee squatted in the low opening and looked at what remained. The skeleton was still wearing moccasins, put on the wrong feet to confuse any *chindi* that might follow the spirit into the darkness of the afterworld. The denim trousers Tsossie had worn had been reduced to scraps of decayed rags, but for some reason the shirt was about half intact. Two buttons still held it across the empty cage of ribs. Chee checked the skeleton's left hand. A finger was missing. Mrs. Musket had said Tsossie had lost a finger. The wind caught the shirttail and blew it against the ribs, revealing the dull silver of leather-strung conchas. The heavy belt that had once encircled a waistline now encircled only a row of whitened vertebrae. Under the concha buckle Chee saw a leather string, the thong of a medicine pouch. Pouch and belt lay just above the socket where the ball joint of Tsossie's thigh bone connected to the pelvic socket. The thigh bone was distorted by a heavy, unnatural growth of scar tissue, an ugly lesion which ran from the joint almost halfway down the heavy bone. It looked very much like the illustration Dr. Huff had pointed out to them in his medical text. Bone cancer. The sort of crazy growth that happens in bone tissue with the metastasis of cell malignancy.

Chee picked up the pouch and pried open the brittle leather.

"It's snowing again," Mary Landon said. She was sitting on the slab outside the cave entrance inspecting the landscape through the binoculars. "And it's getting dark."

"Just another minute or two," Chee said.

The leather broke apart under his fingernail. Inside there was a coating of yellow dust—what once had been sacred pollen. The pollen coated four small fragments of abalone shell, a gallstone taken from some small animal, two feathers, a withered bit of root, and the small stone shape of a mole.

Chee held the mole delicately and polished away the pollen dust. It looked just like the one he had found in Emerson Charley's medicine pouch. Almost identical.

"Jimmy. Somebody's coming."

It was as if they were the same mole. The same amulet. The feel under his fingers was the same. The same blunt legs, the same sloping, pointed snout.

The tone of Mary's voice cut through his concentration more than the meaning of the words. The tone was fear.

"What?" he asked. "Where?"

"There." She pointed over the open hogan roof, past the almost bare cottonwoods, down the track they had followed.

At first he saw nothing. Then a man wearing a navy-blue stocking cap and a heavy black windbreaker trotted into sight. He carried a rifle in his right hand and ran easily, in a low crouch. Chee could see just enough of his face to confirm what he instinctively knew. It was the blond man. In his crouching, careful trot, he was skirting Chee's pickup truck.

"Climb in here," Chee whispered. He helped pull Mary into the blowhole. "It's him," Chee said. "But I don't think he's seen us. He's looking for us around the truck."

"How could he have found us here?" Mary whispered.

"God knows," Chee said. The blond man was kneeling behind a growth of rabbit brush, apparently watching the truck. Chee lifted the binoculars and surveyed the landscape down the track. The man must have driven here and left his vehicle parked somewhere. Chee could see no sign of it. It was probably parked out of sight in the bottom of the arroyo they'd crossed.

Mary found a place behind the bones and the

rocks that had covered them. She sat pressed against the sloping wall, looking first at Chee and then at the skeleton. The blowhole was an elongated circle perhaps six feet along its longest diameter and flattened at the bottom by fallen debris and accumulated dust. The wind had cut into the soft ash no more than four feet. If the man with the rifle learned they were there, the blowhole offered no safety.

Chee spoke in a very low voice. "We stay absolutely still until it gets dark. No motion. No sound. Nothing to attract attention. I want you to ease yourself down as flat as you can get. You're out of sight from where he is now, but do it slowly and carefully. I'm going to lay flat, too. Then he won't be able to see anything in here, even if he tries. Not without climbing up on the slab."

"And we can't see him, either," Mary said in a very faint voice. ' We won't know where he is. We won't be able to do anything to defend ourselves."

"He has the rifle," Chee said. "We don't have any defense against that. Not until it gets dark."

Chee lay on his stomach, his left hand pressed against the tuft beneath him, his right hand gripping the butt of his revolver. Ready to move. There was the smell of dust and ashes in his nostrils. The wind picked up again and hooted through the blowhole opening. Grains of perlite fell against his cheek. The blowhole had become infinitesimally deeper. There was a sound outside. The blond man? The wind? A brushy branch scratching against stone?

Chee struggled against an overwhelming urge to run.

The sound came again. A creaking.

"What was that?" Mary asked. The question had a frantic sound. Panic had come to her a little later than it had to him.

He reached across the bones for her, gripping her leg with his left hand. "The wind," he whispered. "Mary, listen. The way the owl hunts, he sits in a piñon and he hoots. He can't see the rabbits, and they can't see him. And that's the problem for the rabbits. He hoots. And he waits a little to let them think about it, and he hoots again. And the rabbits think. And one of them will think too much. He thinks the owl is getting closer and closer. He thinks the owl has found him. So he makes a run for it, and the owl has her meal for the night."

Mary moved his hand from her leg. "Okay, wise guy," she whispered. "I get your point."

A flurry of snow blew into the hole, the flakes cold against his face. Noises came again and with them a return of panic. He found himself imagining the blond man's face appearing suddenly over the rim of the hole behind the silenced .22 pistol. Chee found his muscles rigid with tension. He forced himself to think of other things. In three weeks he would go to Albuquerque and buy his ticket and report to the FBI Academy. Or he would drive out to the place of Hosteen Nakai and tell his uncle that he was ready to work with him—that Hosteen Nakai could count on him this winter when the calls came to conduct his sings. Which one would it be? He couldn't concentrate on the question. Instead he planned what he would do when darkness came. He would move when there was still a little light. He would find the blond man's car. If the blond man was in it, he would kill him. If he wasn't, then Chee would wait. He waited now, hearing the sound of the wind when it gusted and the sound of Mary breathing when it was silent. He had time now to add what Tsossie's bones and Tsossie's mole had told him to what he had already surmised. The People of Darkness had been murdered. Tsossie had been an unpleasant man, perhaps even a witch. But he had been reduced to bone for a motive that had nothing to do with the anger his unpleasantness had provoked. The motive was mathematical, not emotional. A simple matter of improving the odds against the future. A white man's crime.

Chee felt an impatience to move, to begin the contest. It was much darker, but not quite dark enough. Words from the Stalking Way ran through his memory, his uncle's husky voice singing them, his uncle's stubby fingers tapping rhythm on the pot drum.

I am the Black God, arising with twilight,
    a part of the twilight.
Out from the West, out from the Darkness
    Mountain, a buck of dark flint stands
    out before me.
The best mule game of darkness, it calls to me,
    it hears my voice calling.

Our calls become one in beauty.
  Our prayers become one in beauty.
As I, the Black God, go toward it.
  As the male game of darkness comes toward me.
With beauty before us, we come together.
  With beauty behind us, we come together.
That my arrow may free its sacred breath.
  That my arrow may bring its death in beauty.

The song ran on and on in Chee's mind, a pattern of repetitions, of slightly varied sounds and slightly varied meanings, exorcising the primal dread of death and preparing man and animal for the sacred hunt.

Jimmy Chee was ready. The wind gusted again, sucking into the blowhole, eroding away another thousand infinitesimal grains of ash and moving icy air up Chee's pant leg.

"I'm going now," Chee said. "Stay quiet for a few more minutes, until it's darker, and then slip out and find a sheltered place. But stay within shouting range. When it's safe, I'll call you."

He raised himself to a crouch, surprised at how stiff his muscles had already become.

"I've got a better idea," Mary whispered. "Give me the pistol, and I'll go out and see what I can do. I don't like this being the only one out here who can't shoot back."

Chee grinned. "No; it's my gun. I bought it with my own money."

And with that, he slipped quickly out of the hole,

dropped to the slab, and from the slab to the brushy ground behind it. If the blond man had seen the motion, he hadn't seen it quickly enough to react.

Chee moved as fast as caution allowed. He made a wide circle away from the butte, angling on a course that would cross the little arroyo they'd had trouble traversing. That's where the blond man's vehicle would be and that's where Chee would find the blond man. Somehow, God knew how, he must have guessed the trail ended at the butte and that Chee would be there, and he hadn't risked the noise of trying to grind up the steep arroyo slope. He had parked and come for Chee on foot.

Chee had thought it through very carefully. The blond man had found Chee's pickup truck, but he hadn't found Chee. Hunting him in the brush and boulders around the butte would have been like searching the white man's proverbial haystack for a dangerous needle. So the blond man would opt for another solution. He'd return to his own vehicle and simply wait. When he heard the engine on Chee's pickup start and saw the reflection from Chee's headlights, he would have plenty of time to set up his ambush. The arroyo would be a perfect place for it. Chee's truck creeping down the steep arroyo bank. The blond man shooting Chee through the truck door. Shooting at point-blank range and with plenty of time for as many more shots as were needed if the first one didn't get the job done.

Where Chee reached the arroyo it was much shallower and broader. He hurried up it, moving silently on the sand. Wind and snow had almost stopped, but now the wind rose again, blowing in icy gusts against his face. The right direction for the hunter. Blowing scent and sound away from the prey. Even so, when the arroyo deepened, and when the dim light told him he was within a hundred yards of the point where the track dipped into it, he left the open bottom and moved slowly through the brush.

The vehicle was almost exactly where he'd thought it would be. The blond man had simply nosed it down the arroyo and left it far enough off the track to be out of sight. Chee moved carefully along the extreme edge of the arroyo bottom, slipping from one bit of brush cover to the next. He held the pistol in his right hand at full cock, so that a touch of his thumb to the safety would make it ready to fire.

The eastern sky was totally black now, but the west still filtered a dim twilight through the cloud cover. The blond man's vehicle was a dark-blue GMC pickup truck. From halfway up the arroyo bank where he was crouched, Chee could see the right front and side and look slightly downward into the cab. The cab seemed to be empty. It was empty unless the blond man was prone on the front seat or sitting on the floor. That seemed unlikely. A long willowy wand jutted upward from the back bumper—the antenna of a two-way radio. That was how the blond man had known he could find Chee at Bisti. He had monitored the Navajo Police radio calls.

With that thought came another. What had Chee

said when he talked to Crownpoint? Had he mentioned Mary Landon in that call? Had he even said "we"? Had he said anything that would have told the blond man that Mary was with him? Chee squeezed his eyes shut, concentrating, trying to remember. As always, his memory served. He had said "we." "We're going nine miles northwest of the old trading post. We'll be there until after dark." Those had been his words. So the blond man knew Mary was with him.

Chee slouched back on his heels, his eyes still on the truck, and thought. He considered that the blond man—apparently, at least—was not waiting where Chee's good sense told him the blond man should be waiting. So where was the blond man? He was back at the butte, hunting Chee and Landon. Or he was back at the butte, staked out, watching for them to return to their pickup. Either way he might find Mary, or she might, cold and confused, walk into his trap.

Chee put the pistol carefully on a rock beside his boot. He extracted his billfold, and from the billfold the check Vines had given him. It was perfect for the message. The check itself would tell the blond man that Vines had been in contact with the police. He wrote carefully, trying for legibility in the darkness.

KILLING US WON'T HELP. VINES IS
DEALING WITH FBI. HE GETS OFF LIGHT.

Chee pushed his hand back into his warm glove, picked up the pistol, and moved cautiously to the truck. The door on the driver's side was locked. Chee pulled out the wiper blade and wrapped the check around it securely. If the blond man got back to the truck, he couldn't miss seeing it. It appealed to Chee's Navajo sense of balance, order, and harmony—this business of using the check, the witch's own poison, to turn the evil back against its source. It was the way Changing Woman had taught. Chee trotted off in the darkness toward the butte.

An hour later there was no light at all left in the west. The snow was falling again, still dry, feathery flakes, now drifting almost vertically downward, now whipped by gusts which whistled and moaned around the cliffs of the butte and sent the snow stinging against the skin. Chee had scouted the ground carefully, using his pickup truck as a center and making cautious, time-consuming circles widening around it. He'd moved when the wind blew and crouched motionless, listening, when it dropped into calm. He'd checked every bit of cover that a man in ambush might use to watch the pickup. He'd found nothing. Now he squatted beside a scrubby juniper, thinking. He could see the shape of the pickup against the dark stone of the outcrop. Where could the blond man be? What was he doing? Chee reexamined everything he had been told of the man and everything he had observed himself. He considered the way the man had behaved on the malpais and in the hospital and what Martin had told him of his assassinations. Always meticulous care. Always caution. Never a chance taken. That was the key. No unnecessary chances. No overlooked possibilities. That was why Chee hadn't found him in the two places where the man might logically have been. Because the man had thought it through, had realized that he might have been seen, had realized that Chee might be smart enough to expect a trap or an ambush. Chee frowned into the darkness. The blond man would hardly be floundering around the butte in darkness. He had to be hiding somewhere, waiting. Waiting for what? Waiting for Mary and Chee to get into the pickup and drive into an ambush somewhere? Not if he suspected he had been seen. Then Chee would simply slip into the pickup and radio Crownpoint for assistance. The minute such a call was made, the blond man would be hopelessly trapped. Therefore, the blond man must keep him from his radio. Why isn't he doing that? Chee asked himself. What is to keep me from slipping into the front seat and calling for help? Perhaps he doesn't know that police disconnect the switch that turns on the courtesy light when the door opens. Perhaps he is somewhere, waiting for that flash of light. But no, Chee thought. The blond man would know that. Perhaps he is waiting inside the pickup? No. Chee had left the truck locked. Even if the man picked the lock, hiding inside would be risky.

So how was the blond man protecting himself against the radio call? Chee went over what he knew of the blond man again, incident by incident, from the hospital to the very beginning and the bombing of Emerson Charley's truck in the parking lot. When he reached that, he knew exactly what the blond man had done and what he was waiting for.

He had put a bomb in Chee's pickup. Now he was off somewhere in the darkness, out of the wind and totally unfindable, waiting patiently for Jim Chee and Mary Landon to blow themselves to pieces.

It took Chee only a few minutes to climb the outcrop. From atop that table of stone, he could look directly down into the bed of the truck thirty feet below. It was too dark to be sure, but he could see nothing in the pickup bed that hadn't been there before. If the blond man had placed a bomb, it wasn't likely he had put it in the same place he had used in his effort to kill Emerson Charley. Here, most likely, he would have placed it on the truck frame under the body. If the FBI knew what it was talking about, his bombs detonated when they were moved. Driving over the first bump would do the job. Under the cab, the effects would be certain.

The point where the outcrop jutted from the face of the butte was littered with chunks of fallen stone. Chee picked up one that weighed perhaps twenty pounds and carried it to the edge. He placed himself carefully, over the center of the truck bed. In the same motion he tossed the boulder and jumped backward away from the edge.

The crash of the boulder striking metal was engulfed a minisecond later by a great flash of light and sound. Chee, already off balance, found himself sprawling on hands and knees, his ears ringing and his eyes seeing only the red and white circles imprinted on his retinas by the flash. He lowered himself on the surface of the stone, waiting for sight and hearing to recover.

Soon he could hear a second sound through the receding ringing and see a flickering light through the flash blindness. The truck was burning. At first the flames from the burning gasoline flared above the rim of the outcrop, but they quickly lost their force. Now Chee lay in the darkness looking out across a landscape illuminated by the fire. It was the ideal place to be. When the blond man came to make sure of his victims, Chee would shoot him. Chee lay on his stomach, the cocked pistol held in front of him, waiting.

The wind rose, fanned the flames into a roar, and then died away. The snow drifted straight down again, still dry and feathery. The rock around Chee, blown clear by the most recent gusts, collected another thin layer of snowflakes. Gasoline and oil were almost exhausted now, and the fire fed itself on rubber and upholstery. Chee could smell the rancid black smoke of burning tires and plastic. The landscape the blond man would be crossing was white now. He would be easy to see in the firelight. But the blond man did not come. Through the sound of the fire below him, Chee heard the sound of a starter, and then of a motor, grinding in low gear. Across the ridge where the blond man's pickup had been parked, there appeared a fan of light reflecting in the falling snow. Chee jumped to his feet. The light tilted upward, two visible beams jutting into the snowy sky. The truck was climbing out of the arroyo bottom. But the headlights were pointed away from the butte. The blond man was driving away.

31

THEY BUILT THE FIRE in the crevasse between two of the great fallen slabs in a sheltered
cul-de-sac protected from the wind. Chee had picked
the spot carefully and then had made a walking cir-
cuit, assuring himself that no light, even dimly reflected, was visible. The blond man had driven away
toward the Bisti road. Chee had watched the truck
lights moving eastward until finally they no longer
reappeared through the falling snow. The blond man
probably wouldn't return. There was no reason for
him to do so. But he might.

Now, finally, they were out of the wind. Mary
Landon sat across from him, back against the verti-
cal stone, her denimed legs stretched straight in
front of her. Above them the wind gusted past the
butte top with a hooting noise. Between these walls
of fallen stone, it only caused the fire to flicker. But
Mary shivered and hugged herself.

"I think it was a mistake," she said, "leaving that
note about Mr. Vines."

"Why?"

"Because," Mary said. "Because maybe he'll go and shoot Vines—and you don't know for sure Vines killed anyone. You don't have any proof."

"I know for sure," Chee said.

"You don't have anything to prove it with. You're not a judge."

Chee thought about that. The firelight was red, burning the rosin of dead piñon. It reflected on Mary Landon's face, casting deep shadows where her hair fell across her forehead.

"Yes," Chee said, "I am a judge. If the blond man kills Vines, then that's justice. But he's not going to kill Vines. He won't have time. He can't get there tonight because of the weather. If we get three inches of snow down here, there'll be two feet of it up on Mount Taylor. The road won't be open until they get a snowplow on it—and that won't be until tomorrow morning. They'll be using the snowplows where there's more traffic."

"Still, you don't have any right to . . ."

"We don't have much violence, we Navajos. What there is is mostly associated with witchcraft. Changing Woman taught us how to cope with the Navajo Wolves. We turn the evil around so it works against the witch."

"But first you have to know for sure he's the witch," Mary said.

The snow started again, larger flakes now. The wind moaned around the butte top and the snowflakes eddied and swirled above them, lit by the redness of the fire. Some settled into the cul-de-sac. They landed on Chee's knee, on Mary's hair, on stone surfaces. Some drifted into the fire and vanished—cold touched by the magic of heat.

It was going to be a long, frigid night, and there was nothing that could be done until there was a little light. When it was light, the pipeline companies would be scouting their collection systems to make sure the abrupt drop in temperature had cracked no exposed metal, separated no joints, jammed no valves. The little slow-flying planes would be up looking for signs of gas leaks. Whatever those signs were. Spurts of blowing dust, Chee guessed. He remembered they had crossed the El Paso Natural Gas trunkline between Bisti and the butte. When dawn came, they would walk to it and build a smoky fire and wait to be spotted. Until then there was nothing to be done, except help time pass, avoid freezing, and think.

"I am born a Slow Talking People," Chee said. "I'm also a member of the Red Forehead Clan because my father was one. And I'm connected with the Mud Clan, because my uncle—the one teaching me to be a singer—he's married into the Muds. All of those clans have the same tradition. To become a witch, to cross over from Navajo to Navajo Wolf, you have to break at least one of the most serious taboos. You have to commit incest, or you have to kill a close relative. But there's another story, very old, pretty much lost, which explains how First Man became a witch. Because he was first, he didn't have relatives to destroy. So he figured out a magic way to violate the strongest taboo of all. He destroyed himself and recreated himself, and that's the way he got the powers of evil."

"I never heard about that," Mary said. "I thought for a minute you were changing the subject. But you're not, are you?"

"I'm not," Chee said. "Lebeck decided to be a witch. He destroyed himself. And he came back."

Mary was frowning at him. "Lebeck? The geologist at the oil well?"

"Yes; the geologist," Chee said. "Think about what we know. We know the oil well was drilled through uranium, because the Red Deuce is now mining that deposit where the oil well stood. Lebeck was what they call the 'well logger'—the one who inspects samples of the rock they're drilling through and maps the deposits. Very shallow, maybe down just fifty feet or so, the bit goes through pitchblende, a thick layer of the very richest uranium ore. So Lebeck suddenly knows something that's worth hundreds of millions of dollars. How can he cash it in? He can cash it in only if this oil lease is allowed to expire. Then he can file his own mineral lease claim. So he falsifies the log."

Mary was leaning forward, intent. "Hey," she said. "You looked at the log. Did he? Why didn't you tell me? How could you tell?"

Chee made a wry face. "I couldn't tell," he said. "I checked out that log and a couple of other ones from other wells drilled in Valencia County, and they all looked about alike. The oil companies were all looking for a shallow oil sand, just down about two thousand feet. I was looking for God knows what down at the bottom of the well, down at the end where they were deciding to shoot the tubing with the nitro. I didn't know what I was looking for, and I didn't see anything."

"But you should have seen something," Mary said slowly. "You should have seen they'd drilled through the uranium ore."

"Exactly!" Chee said. "I've heard that Red Deuce deposit is a couple of hundred feet deep. It should have been noted on the log." Chee felt an overpowering urge to smoke. He hadn't had a possibility of lighting a cigaret since the blond man's arrival at the butte. He fished out a Pall Mall, offered it to Mary. She shook her head. He lit it.

"Those things will kill you," Mary said.

"Actually, I think now he must have falsified the log twice. Once when they drilled through the ore and again at the end. I think they found the oil sand they were looking for, and Lebeck put it down as something else and had them drill right through it. Or maybe he had the log show they were drilling into a geological formation which should be below the oil sand—which would mean the sand didn't exist at this particular place. Anyway, he wanted them to shut down the well and let the lease lapse, so he could get a lease on it himself. If they struck oil, the lease would be renewed by the oil company and he would never get the uranium. So when the company decided to shoot the well, Lebeck must have known there was a good chance that would start the oil flowing. He couldn't risk that." Chee inhaled a lungful of smoke and let it trickle from between his lips. It made blue swirls in the slowly moving air, drifting upward while the white flakes drifted down. Far above at the butte top, the north wind, the evil wind, began hooting again. Chee puffed out the last of the smoke, destroying the pattern with his breath. "And so Lebeck decided to blow everything, and everyone, sky high. Lebeck decided to become a witch."

He glanced at Mary.

"To die, or seem to die, and to come back as B. J. Vines," she said.

"Yes," Chee said.

"But when the nitro truck arrived, something went wrong. Dillon Charley's crew didn't show up for work."

"How did Dillon Charley know?"

"The Lord Peyote told him in a vision," Chee said. "Or perhaps Lebeck warned him—which I doubt. Or perhaps Dillon Charley saw things that made him nervous. I think Charley was a very perceptive man. Mrs. Vines told me that her husband and Dillon Charley were friends—had a sort of rapport. Perhaps that was already true when Vines was Lebeck." Chee shrugged. "Who knows? Lord Peyote, or nervousness about nitroglycerin, or what? Anyway, he didn't show up that day, and he warned his crew away. I think Lebeck wanted them all there. No one else around here knew him. No one else would recognize him as Vines. But he didn't have any choice. The nitro truck came. He had to act then or never."

"How did he do it?" Mary asked.

"I have to guess. Obviously he left the rig. I'd say he probably got far enough away to be safe, and he had a rifle and fired a shot into the nitro bottle at the proper moment."

Mary Landon shivered again and hugged herself. "And then he just walked away, so he'd be counted among the dead. Didn't he have a family? A mother and father? People who loved him?"

"I don't know anything about Lebeck," Chee said.

"And then to come back here. Wouldn't he be afraid someone would recognize him?"

"Probably nobody knew him, or had even seen him much. Just the well crew. It was an isolated place. Hardly a road then, and the crew would have lived out at the well, where nobody saw them. And then he stayed away two years. Maybe a little more. Long enough for the mineral lease to expire. Long enough to grow a heavy beard. Who knows—maybe he did something else to change his looks. I said we didn't know anything about Lebeck, but we do know a little. You get into the paratroops by volunteering. And once he was in, he won two top decorations for courage. So I guess he wasn't afraid of taking chances. Or of killing, either. He must have done a lot of it." Chee paused, thinking about it. "I guess he knew he'd have some more to do."

"The People of Darkness," Mary said.

"Yeah. He couldn't count on Dillon Charley forgetting him."

"You think Dillon Charley saw Vines and recognized him as Lebeck?"

"Maybe. But I'll bet Lebeck didn't wait for that to happen. I'll bet he went looking for him. Maybe he told Charley the Lord Peyote had given him a vision, too. Or maybe he just offered him a job, money, so forth. He'd know Charley wouldn't tell the sheriff anything—not with the way Gordo was harassing him and his church. And besides, Charley wasn't going to live very long."

"Lebeck knew Dillon Charley had cancer?"

"Lebeck knew Charley was going to have cancer," Chee corrected. "That black rock, it must be pitchblende. When the oil well bit drilled through it, Lebeck recognized pitchblende, and that's the hottest kind of natural uranium deposit. He didn't put it on the log, but he saved a piece of the core to test and make sure. And then he kept it because he saved mementos, and this one was going to change his life. Maybe he already knew it was going to be useful to him."

"You're losing me," Mary said. "How do you know it's pitchblende? I never heard of it. How do you know so much about it?"

"Out here everybody is prospecting half the time," Chee said. "You learn about minerals, and mostly you learn about uranium-bearing minerals. I should have thought of it before. I think if we get a mineralogist to check those rock samples and those mole amulets, we're going to find they're radioactive. Vines gave Charley the mole knowing he would carry it in his medicine pouch—hanging from his waist under his clothing right against the groin." .

"Dillon Charley, and Tsossie, and Begay, and Sam, and all of them," Mary said. She shivered again.

"He didn't overlook much," Chee said. "I think Dillon Charley must have been the first to die, and Vines got the body and buried it, just in case an autopsy would show something. But Navajos don't have much interest in bodies, and the authorities don't have much interest in dead Navajos, and people got scattered out, so after Dillon Charley it wasn't worth the trouble, I guess. It looked like he could quit worrying. Everybody on that work crew who had ever seen him as Lebeck was dead, or soon would be. Nothing to worry about for years."

"Not until Emerson Charley gets cancer," Mary Landon said.

"I think that's right," Chee said. "Old Dillon was a pretty important religious leader, and people like that sometimes try to pass it along to their children. I guess he gave Emerson his medicine bundle, hoping he'd become the peyote chief, and one day, years later, Emerson decides to revive the cult. He starts wearing old Dillon's mole, and of course he gets sick. . . ."

Mary was leaning forward now. "And Vines gets nervous," she said. "Now it's 1980, and Vines doesn't want Emerson checking into a modern cancer research center, where he's sure to undergo an autopsy, and so he hires somebody to kill him."

"And to steal the body," Chee said.

"And probably to get the mole back. But the blond man missed the mole."

"And Tomas Charley was too suspicious. The Navajos around Mount Taylor may not know a lot about radioactive pathology, but they could count up the fact that people who associated with Vines seemed to die. They knew he was a witch. When Emerson Charley's truck was bombed, Tomas was suspicious. He wanted to prove Vines was a witch. He broke in and stole the box, and all Mrs. Vines knew was that the box was extremely important to Vines, so she asked me to get it back. I think she wanted to know Vines' secret."

The snow was falling more heavily now, drifting almost straight down out of an abruptly windless sky.

"Can't we build that fire a little higher?" Mary asked.

"A little," Chee said. He moved two chunks of piñon trunk into the blaze.

"You can't prove any of this, can you?" Mary said. It wasn't a question.

"I won't have to," Chee said. "I told the blond man. Tomorrow we'll tell Gordo Sena. Sena won't need proof either."

32

CHEE PASSED THE WORD to Sheriff Sena via
the radio in an El Paso Natural Gas Company helicopter. The copter had found them where the EPNG
collector pipe bridges Nagasi Wash. They had built
a fire in the brush that flourishes there, and not ten
minutes after the greasy smoke spiraled into the sky,
the little Bell had puttered over the rise. The pilot
was a young man with a scarred nose, a walrus mustache, and the emblem of a First Cavalry Division
gunship unit sewed on his greasy flying jacket. He
had already spotted their bombed pickup truck, and
circled it curiously, and he was ready to believe
Chee's story of a police emergency.

Chee told the sheriff's dispatcher at Grants no
more than Gordo Sena would need to know.

"Tell him the man who killed Tomas Charley is
headed for B. J. Vines' house. Tell him that Vines
hired the man, and tell him that Vines' real name is
Carl Lebeck."

"Lee what?" the dispatcher asked.

"Lebeck," Chee said. "Be sure to get that right. Carl Lebeck." Except for describing the truck, and the blond man, Chee offered no more details. They would be redundant. Gordo Sena had lived for thirty years with the details of that oil well explosion burning in his mind. He'd know instantly who Lebeck was, and he was smart enough to put it all together. The dispatcher had said Sena had left for the Anaconda Mine. The same road led through the fringes of the Laguna reservation toward the high slopes of Mount Taylor and Vines' place. About fifteen miles, Chee guessed, compared to the sixty they had to cover in the helicopter. But that last mile or two would be impassable to something on wheels. Sena would have to walk in. Chee would get there first.

The thought excited him. At one level he was afraid of the blond man. At another, he longed to find him. His broken rib ached, as it had ached all morning. But it was more than vengeance. The man had shot him once. He had twice hunted Chee down to kill him. The memory still rankled—of the interminable minutes spent on the metal duct above the hospital ceiling, of the helpless panic in the blowhole. Now he was the stalker. He tried to analyze the feeling. Expectant? Exultant? Something between, and something more. There was a mixture of fear and of the remembered childhood feeling of the hunt. The smell of smoke, of boiling coffee, the forest scents carried on the predawn dew. His uncle greeting the sun with the dawn chant and blessing them all with the sacred pollen and singing the final song to call the spirits of the deer. Through the scarred, oil-smeared Plexiglas he could see the Turquoise Mountain rushing toward them, its upper slopes a virginal white, glittering in the sunlight against a sky swept clean by the night's storm. The thump of the copter blades covered the words as he repeated the Stalking Song. Perhaps Mary heard them, jammed as she was between him and the pilot. She glanced at him curiously.

They found the blond man's pickup truck about three twisting miles below the Vines house. Chee examined it through his binoculars, and the tracks told a story that was easy to read. The truck had slid off the narrow forest service road, losing traction on an upslope, where its spinning rear wheels moved sideways into the ditch. The driver had emerged, walked uphill several hundred yards, and then returned to the truck. He'd done this while the snow was still falling heavily, and his tracks were half-filled depressions. Later, when the snow was no longer falling, he had emerged again, walking uphill through snow that now was perhaps two feet deep. The new tracks were easy to follow, but there was no reason to follow them. They would lead to Vines' house.

The only question was whether they had yet reached the house. How fast could the blond man struggle uphill through deep snow? A mile an hour? At the butte the snowfall had stopped about 4:00 A.M. On the mountain, it would have lasted longer. Perhaps until 5:00 or 6:00.

"Let's take the shortest way to Vines'," Chee said. "When we're there, get close to the ground and try to keep behind the trees. They'll hear us, but I don't want them to know where you're letting me off."

"Letting you off?" Mary said. "You're out of your mind. We'll wait for the sheriff. He can't get away now."

"No," Chee said. "There's something I have to do."

The copter settled in a great cloud of feathery snow behind a cluster of blue spruce which screened off the garage. Chee dropped into a snowbank deeper than his knees and stood blinded for a moment while the copter pulled up and away. Then he ran, floundering, to the stone wall of the garage. The blond man, and Vines, and Mrs. Vines, anyone in the house, would have heard the copter, but they couldn't have seen it, and they wouldn't know it had dropped him. Still, he'd be careful. He stood against the wall, remembering the layout of the house. It sat with its back into the mountain slope, looking outward across the great panorama below. But the view was limited. Behind the house, the wall was low and windowless, and in many places one could step from the mountainside to the tile roof. Chee trotted around the garage. The tombstones of Dillon Charley and the first and faithful Mrs. Vines wore high white hats of snow. Behind the house, he stopped to listen. The stillness was almost total—the silence of a windless morning on a mountain buried under new white insulation. From somewhere back in the forest, a fir limb bent and gave up its bushels of snow with a sibilant sound. From the house, only silence.

Thirty feet ahead there was a doorway. Perhaps a laundry room, or some other sort of utility entrance. Chee moved toward it cautiously, keeping close to the wall, with the pistol, cocked, in his right hand. He tried the knob. Unlocked.

Over the roof he heard the sound of the copter. It was approaching fast. The sound peaked, receded, and returned. First Cavalry was creating a distraction for him, Chee realized. Mary's idea, probably. He pulled the door open and slipped inside.

The room seemed almost totally dark. He stood, back to the door, giving his eyes a chance to make the adjustment from the brilliance of sunlight off snow to the interior gloom. He was in a sort of washroom/supply room. Down a short, narrow hall he could see into the kitchen. His ears told him absolutely nothing. The house was as silent as the snow outside. But something reached his nose. Acrid. The smell of blue smoke produced by gunpowder. Chee leaned against the edge of the clothes drier, unlaced his wet boots and removed them. He moved silently down the hall, placing his stockinged feet noiselessly. The kitchen was empty. It was lighter. The room was lit by a row of small high windows and more light came in from the broad doorway, which opened into what seemed to be a game room. Chee moved through the kitchen, back to the wall, trying to see into the adjoining room without being seen himself. He edged past the door of what was probably a pantry. Then he froze.

From behind him came a quick gasping sound a quick release of breath, a quick intake of breath. Someone was standing behind the door, inches away from his back.

Chee slid away from the door. He stood beside it. Listening. His pistol was cocked. The safety off. He squatted just to the left of the door, facing it. He reached across his body with his left hand and gripped the knob. Then he thought. This was not where he would find the blond man—not hiding in a closet. He heard the clamor of the helicopter again from the front of the house, and he jerked the door open.

The Acoma woman stood there. She looked startled, but she made no sound.

Chee put a finger to his lips, signaling silence. "Where is everyone?" he whispered in English.

The Acoma woman stared at his pistol. It was pointed at her stomach. Chee lowered it.

"A blond man came here," Chee said. "Is he here?"

She seemed not to understand. She appeared to be stunned. "Where is everyone?" Chee repeated.

The woman released another gasp of breath. *"El brujo esta muerto,"* she said. That was all she would say. She said it twice, and then she turned abruptly and walked silently down the hallway and disappeared into the laundry room. Chee heard the outside door open. And then close.

"The witch is dead." Did she mean the blond man? Did she mean Vines? Not Mrs. Vines. She had used the masculine noun. The dead witch was male.

Chee found him in Vines' study. He sat behind the great desk, still upright because the swivel chair had been tilted slightly backward, and the impact of the bullet had pushed his head against the leather cushion. The light from the sunny snow outside streamed through the shutters and lit his face and showed a spot low on the forehead just above the bridge of his nose. It hadn't bled much, but a trickle had run down across his cheek and into his white beard. B. J. Vines' eyes were still open, but the witch was forever dead.

Where was the blond man? Chee stood just inside the door, back to the wall, listening. He heard nothing. The copter had gone now. Had it landed? Vines' dead face wore a look of shocked surprise. He had seen death coming. A tigress looked over his shoulder, her glittering glass eyes staring at Chee. Where was the blond man? Chee found himself thinking instead of B. J. Vines' head mounted among those of the other predators, the blue eyes glittering. The blond man might have left. He would hardly stay after he had accomplished his purpose. Chee moved quickly around the desk. He put his finger against Vines' throat. The skin was still soft and warm. He touched the bloody streak that ran down the side of the nose. Not even sticky yet. Vines had been dead only minutes. No more than five or ten. The blond man was close. Then where was Rosemary Vines? Perhaps she was away from home.

Chee stood beside the desk, watching the door,

listening. What would the blond man do? The copter thudded close again, hovering in front of the house. Mary trying to help. He remembered the blond man's rifle. Stay away, Mary. Stay out of range. She was a woman among women. She made him happy. She was a friend. She made him feel like singing. She deserved nothing but beauty all around her. But now, stay away. The blond man must be in the house. Close. Doing what? Looking for servants? Making sure he'd leave no one alive to report this visit? Chee's eyes rested on the telephone. The line would be cut. He picked up the receiver, expecting deadness. Instead he heard the buzzing dial tone. He dialed 0. It rang, and a woman's voice said, "Operator. Can I help you?"

"Sorry," Chee whispered. He hung up. Why had the blond man left the telephone intact? He hadn't got to it yet. Then he heard the sound. Someone coughed. And coughed again.

The blond man was sitting on the floor of the entrance foyer, his shoulder against the massive door. Blood was everywhere. It splashed across the polished wood, it soaked the blond man's trousers, it spread in a still-growing stain across the patterned ceramic tiles of the floor. A pistol lay in the blood, black, with the long cylinder of a silencer on its barrel. The blond man coughed again. He glanced at Chee, then focused his eyes on him. He moved his lips, tentatively. Then he said:

"It's cold."

Chee could see what had happened. The shot had

hit the blond man as he reached the door. One of Vines' hunting rifles, probably. Something big. The slug had torn through him from the back, splashing the door with blood. It had broken the blond man as a stick is broken.

"Is there someplace warm?" the blond man asked.

"Maybe the fireplace," Chee said. He put his pistol in its holster, walked through the blood, and squatted beside the blond man. He put an arm under his legs and an arm behind his shoulders and lifted him—carefully because the blood was slippery under his socks, carefully because the man was dying.

In the big room, a log fire had burned itself down to flickering coals in the fireplace. Chee knelt in front of it and put the blond man on the skin of the polar bear. The man's back was broken somewhere between the shoulder blades. The blond man's head rolled toward the fire. His voice was small.

"There's this detective agency," he said. "Webster. In Encino. He's going to find my mother. She'll know about the cemetery. She'll come and get me."

"All right," Chee said. "Don't worry."

"I thought I killed him," Rosemary Vines said. She was standing in the doorway, holding a long-barreled rifle. It was pointed roughly in Chee's direction.

"You did," Chee said. "It takes a few minutes."

Mrs. Vines' face was bloodless. The lipstick she wore made a grotesque contrast against chalky skin.

"Did you know who your husband was?" Chee asked.

Rosemary Vines stared past him, her eyes on the blond man. She's in shock, Chee thought. She didn't even hear me.

"I knew he'd had another life somewhere," she said slowly. "I suspected that even before we were married. He loved to talk about himself, but not back before a certain time. Earlier than that—when he was a boy, when he was in college, any of that time before he'd come out here and found his mine—any time before that it was all very vague. So he had to be hiding something. And finally he admitted he had his secrets. But he'd never tell me what. I told him it had to be criminal or he wouldn't be ashamed of it. But he'd just laugh."

On the pelt of the dead polar bear, the blond man was now quite motionless. Rosemary Vines still stared at his body, the rifle still ready.

"I knew it was in his safe. In his box. It had to be. That's the way B.J. was. Everything he did, he had to keep the evidence. Heads. Pelts. Photographs. He was compulsive about it. Like he had to have proof it had happened. He wouldn't take twenty-five years of his life and just throw it away. If I could get the box before he got back, there'd be things in there to tell me who B.J. had been when he was young. And there'd be something to tell me what it was he was so ashamed of."

The thought brought something like animation to her face—a look of triumph anticipated. It was a sort of smile. "Ashamed of, or afraid of," Mrs. Vines said, still smiling.

Jim Chee looked away from her, away from the body, and the white fur stained with red. Through the great soaring expanse of glass that lit the room he could see only sky and snow. Blue and white purity. Such beauty should have aroused in Jim Chee an exultation. Now he felt nothing. Only numb fatigue and a kind of sickness.

But he knew the cause, and the cure. Changing Woman had taught them about it when she formed the first clans of the Dinee from her own skin. The strange ways of strange people hurt the spirit, turned the Navajo away from beauty. Returning to beauty required a cure. He would go tomorrow to Hosteen Nakai and ask him to arrange an Enemy Way, to gather family, the interlinked relatives of the Slow Talking Dinee and the Red Forehead Dinee—the brothers and sisters of his blood, his friends, his supporters. Then there would be another eight days for the songs and the poetry and the sand paintings to recreate the past and restore the spirit.

He would persuade Hosteen Nakai that Mary, too, should undergo the blessing even though she was not born Dinee. The arrangements would take weeks—picking the site, spreading the word, getting the proper singer, arranging the food. But when it was over, he would go again with beauty all around him.